To Joe

(signature)

ET

LIE
LO

The Epic of Cougran

Adventures in Raoolia

Written by Eric Tilden
Edited by Pamela and Eric Tilden

Second Edition

Copyright © 2007. All rights reserved. No portion of this book may be reproduced without written permission from the author, except for the brief quotation in critical reviews and articles.

ISBN: 978-0-6151-6043-6

Published By:
P*JET * IMAGES
http://www.pjetimages.com

Printing and book manufacturing by Lulu, Inc.
http://www.lulu.com

This is a work of fiction. All names, places, characters, incidents, and images are the product of the author's imagination or borrowed from the public domain (i.e. Minotaur, Greek Mythology). Any resemblance to actual persons, living or dead is purely coincidental.

Printed in the United States of America.

The power of choice
is our only guard against letting in evil...

The Epic of Cougran *Adventures in Raoolia*

Prologue.. ix
Map of Cougran.. xiii
Book 1: Tragedy at BellBour........................... 1
1.   Pursuit.. 2
2.   BellBour Village..................................... 9
3.   Quest.. 15
4.   Bait and Switch..................................... 21
5.   Consummation and Destruction...... 26
Book 2: The Journey to Shven-Shong........... 30
6.   Discovery... 32
7.   Hierarchy... 37
8.   On the Move.. 45
9.   Power.. 51
10.   Manipulation... 57
Intermission... 66
Book 3: March of the Minotaurs.................... 68
11.   Introspection... 69
12.   Annihilation... 75
13.   The Siege Part I.................................... 81
14.   The Siege Part II................................... 85
15.   The Siege Part III.................................. 89
Book 4: The Ripple Effect................................ 93
16.   Deconstruction..................................... 94
17.   Ambush!.. 98
18.   Deforestation and Rebirth.............. 102
19.   The Fruit of Evil.................................. 108
20.   The Summit of Nidia.......................... 112
Book 5: Expedition... 117
21.   Aerial Expedition............................... 118
22.   Meeting of the Minds........................ 124
23.   Mystery of the Red Rain.................. 128
24.   Raoolian Raid...................................... 132
25.   Another Piece of the Puzzle............ 136
Book 6: Invasion.. 141
26.   Findings... 142
27.   Inside the Nidian High Council........ 146
28.   Deployment.. 150
29.   Springing the Trap............................. 154
30.   A Mixed Victory.................................. 160
Book 7: Retaliation.. 164
31.   Small Step Forward........................... 165
32.   Voyage Home....................................... 169
33.   In the Navy... 173
34.   Infiltration.. 178
35.   Out of the Woodwork........................ 182
Epilogue.. 186
Appendix... I
Shougren Calendar.. III
Visual Narrative.. V

Prologue

In a distant galaxy, millions of light-years from Earth, a blue-white star was born. Over time, gas and dust collided and contracted to form 12 planets. On the sixth and seventh planets, life evolved. Cougran, the sixth planet, evolved into a seven continent, tropical world with abundant life on land and in the sea. The seventh planet, called Colwoof, is a colder world. Ice and snow cover the top and bottom third of the planet, its equatorial region is temperate with four distinct seasons.

On Cougran, two feline-based humanoid races arose, the Carcalians and later a mutant race, the Tigrens. Tigrens are born with a mutated recessive gene that enables them to enlarge themselves at will, from the normal three and a half feet to ten feet tall! Their bodies are all muscle, and rage and aggression rule their emotions.

At the equivalent pubescent age, Tigrens get their ability to metamorphosize and become very fierce individuals. The violent and volatile nature of the Tigren teen led to the deaths of many Carcalian families. The Tigrens wandered off into the wilderness and formed wild populations, creating fear among the Carcalian communities.

This cycle of terror continued for generations until one day, a Tigren learned self-control. Instead of killing his Carcalian family, he established an Academy for mutant Carcalians like himself, called the Shou Clan, and began calling his race Tigren. The Shou Clan was the first Academy that established the tradition of training Tigrens from an early age. Tigrens were easy to single out at an early age, for when they were born, a symbol, caused by a recessive gene, appeared on their back.

Over time, this recessive gene built up in the population so that at this point in history, twenty-five percent of the population is born Tigren. The Shou Clan Leaders decided to take 6 Masters and spread out over the seven continents, to absorb local Tigren populations. Over several thousand years, it became normal for Tigrens to be given over to the clans at birth. Wild populations were believed extinct.

Tigrens are trained in the martial arts, hand-to-hand combat, tracking, weapons, military-style warfare, self-control, and stealth. This training helps the normally aggressive Tigrens channel their natural violent tendencies, and it prevents them from killing Carcalians. Unfortunately, their mutation has left them born sterile, so they still must rely upon Carcalians to perpetuate their population. Each mating season, during the 8th month of the year, called Estrella, the Intercontinental Games occur during the first 12 weeks of the 13-week month, celebrating the birth cycle of both species. The Academies host and compete in the Games, which are martial arts matches similar to our Olympics.

To finish off the month, the Carcalians celebrate their Mating Ritual during this 13th week. The Ritual calls for five days of combat, five days of recuperation, and three days of mating. The Carcalians go through a metamorphosis also, but on a smaller scale. The normally 3 and a half foot males grow to be 5 foot 10 inches tall, and the normally 3 foot females grow to be 5 foot 6 inches. Each gender becomes more cat-like, growing canine teeth, claws, and for females, multiple sets of breasts (after conception). Carcalian males go from basic muscle groups to a massive muscular bodybuilder-like beast, fierce and ready to fight with other males for the right to mate with one female.

Our story takes place on the Continent of Raoolia, in the year 5049, the first month of the 13-month year, called Shou after the Shou Clan. Raoolia is located in the Southern Hemisphere, about 3,000 miles south of the equator. Lake Leopold is located ¼ of the way inland from the eastern shore. The Raoolen River cuts the continent in half, flowing from the Sybeerian Ocean to the Straits of Raoonada, through the lake. A small village called BellBour resides along the Raoolen River, west of Lake Leopold.

Several miles to the west of BellBour Village, on the northern side of the river, lays Shalou City. Several hundred miles northwest of that major city, at the tip of Raoolia, is the location of the Shven-Shong. The Shven-Shong is the local Tigren Clan of the continent.

The Planet Cougran

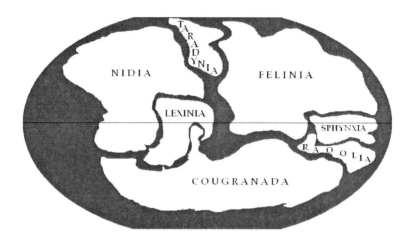

The planet Cougran is the sixth planet to a blue-white giant star in a galaxy 75 million light-years from Earth. This planet is a tropical world. Its temperature is such that there are no polar regions. The main intelligent inhabitants are at the technology level of Ancient Rome. They sail the seas, they fight with spears, swords, shields, and bows and arrows. They ride animals to get from place to place, including mystical creatures that do not exist in our world.

Welcome to
The Epic of Cougran...

Book 1: Tragedy at BellBour Village

Chapter List

Chapter 1:	Pursuit..	2
Chapter 2:	BellBour Village..............................	9
Chapter 3:	Quest...	15
Chapter 4:	Bait and Switch...............................	21
Chapter 5:	Consummation and Destruction.....	26

Chapter 1: Pursuit

Shou 8, 5049

It was a crisp morning. No movement to the east, that's where I saw them last. I didn't think they still existed. As far back as anyone could remember, the Academies provided a place for them to harness their savage nature. Yet here I was, running for my life through the forest. They must have picked up my scent near the lake, where I had been camping for the last three nights. If I'm lucky, I can leave this cave and make it to BellBour Village by nightfall, as long as I don't run into any more of those Tigrens.

Liotoch slowly inched himself out of the cave, listening for the slightest indication of pursuit. He sniffed the air, and when he was sure that the 'coast was clear,' he ran off through the forest, heading west to BellBour. He knew that BellBour would be a safe haven from those wild terrorists. The Tigrens would never follow him into civilization. Wild Tigrens were rumored to hate settlements.

"We shall see," he thought aloud.

Some distance from the cave, Liotoch noticed a blam-bird hopping about in the trees, no doubt searching for some tasty fruit to feast on. It had been many hours since Lio had eaten, as if running for his life allotted time to think about food! He hadn't seen 'hide nor hair' of the Tigrens since he ducked into that cave early this morning. Lio decided that since he wasn't in any immediate danger, it wouldn't hurt to climb the nearest Stig tree and help himself to a sample of the delectably sweet fruit. After all, if those Tigrens had tracked him, he'd be relatively safe up in the branches, since the Tigrens were too bulky to climb trees.

The rage flowing like a river, their senses keen and sharp as razors, the Tigrens plowed through the forest like a battalion of tanks, uprooting bushes and snapping branches effortlessly. The pack often hunted separately, increasing the chances of survival, and decreasing the chances of being discovered, but not this time. A Carcalian had entered their territory, degrading the sacred forest, like the other Carcalians have done planet-wide. They send a few at first, and then thousands come, tear down the forest, suck-up all the resources, and destroy the serenity. This could not be permitted to happen, not again, not ever!!!

Fruit from the Stig tree, called yellato, has a hard, outer shell that cleaves quite easily when bitten with one's canines, yielding a very sweet and juicy pulp and one small seed in the center. The seed, when crushed, can be made into baked goods, or a golden dye for clothing. As I was taking my first bite, I heard pekalls in the distance, taking to the sky in droves, as if being spooked by something –

"OH NO!"

Crashing and smashing sounded in the distance. They had found him!

"I have to go now!" he said, in utter fear.

Leaping from branch to branch, he scurried like a squirrel, trying to get a running head start. If they caught him, he could end up as dinner and a left boot. These Tigrens had already killed his shaklow and had eaten it raw. They were definitely not to be messed with!

"Wait! Shut-up you oafs! I hear something!" said Denzcan. "Up about ten strides...he's in the trees!!! After him!"

Rumbling and crashing through the forest, thousands of fleeing animals nearly trampled the small Carcalian, and then...silence! Good! I'll get ahead of them and safety will envelop me like the light from our blue sun, Estatia. Then, once again, crashing, rumbling, and this time I heard them shouting. They're so close now. I had better find another hiding place quick, before they find...

Just then, all the energy was zapped from my limbs, and I fell from the trees, 15 feet to the ground, with a thud. The ground and I were inseparable. What happened? Why couldn't I move?

Small trickles of strength returned to my neck. I elevated it slightly, and noticed a rabball hole just a few inches away. I pulled my body into the hole with every ounce of energy that I had left. When I fell into the hole, I pulled a rope that closed the hatch.

"Ha! I got him!" said Fent. "These Felowitzers we stole from the Academy really work!! He should be one stride ahead of us, in that thick bunch of bushes." They strode ahead, to capture their quarry, but when they arrived at the approximate location, the Carcalian was nowhere to be found!

"Well, where'd he go? Carcalian's just don't up and disappear, especially when they drop like a rock out of the trees! Fan out, look under every bush and thicket, I want that Carcalian found!" barked Denzcan.

After what seemed like forever, Lio regained his strength, enough, at least, to get up and find a way out. There were three ways he could go, up and be killed, left into the darkness, or right into the darkness. Some choice! Well, the way to BellBour was left, so that's the way he would go. So he picked himself up,

5

dusted himself off, and set off to what lay ahead. He decided that death would have to come later, much later, he hoped.

Lio is a male Carcalian. He has red-orange fur covering his back, arms and legs, neck and tail. His belly is a pale yellow, as are his hands, feet, and face. His mane, which is shoulder-length, like all males, is sandy yellow. Because he is only 6 years old, he has only mated once. After every successful mating season, when they revert to their short height, both genders' head hair darkens as an indication of their experience.

At the age of 15, the mating cycle ends, their hair remains black, and they are forever metamorphosized. The first mating period is the most traumatic on the body. The 3 ½ foot males grow to be 5 foot 10 inches high. Their chests, biceps, legs, and back triple in muscle mass. The abdominal muscles ripple into a 12 pack, three columns, and four rows of ripped muscle!! Claws turn black, and grow to be an inch long. Their sense of smell becomes extremely acute and the only thing they can think about is the need to fight.

Female Carcalians metamorphosize into larger and fiercer versions of themselves, growing to be five foot six inches tall. They also grow longer, retractable claws, bushier head hair, rounded hips, and a pair of rounded breasts over their upper teats. They pick out several potential mates to fight in the ring for the right to reproduce. The winner takes the female upstairs to the loft to recover from the fight and to copulate. While the mating itself is the perfect balance to the trauma, the most devastating thing is the change in appearance. One's facial features elongate, ears lengthen, canine teeth grow, their muzzle extends, and hair grows all around the mouth. It is a horrific sensation!

After mating week is over, the males revert to normal and go about their lives. The females that mate have a 100% pregnancy rate, lasting six weeks. After conception, the females grow three more pairs of breasts so they may suckle up to eight pups at a time, which is a typical litter size. If they happen to have a Tigren pup, the infant is whisked away after birth to be raised in the Tigren Academy.

The females revert to normal after their Carcalian pups are weaned off their milk at 6 months. The females raise the pups until they are two years old, then the father teaches them the family business for three years, and the cubs are then sent out to live on their own. Females can choose to mate or they can stay home during that week and remain secluded.

After walking for several hours, Lio noticed another exit hole above, the only light in this underground labyrinth. He poked his head up, and looked around, no Tigrens. Good! He took off to the west. It was only a short distance to sanctuary.

As the sun set in the western horizon, he could see the lights of the village in the distance. He had made it! He was alive!

Denzcan, Fent, Sando, Teelor, Wensha, Babbel, and Puven, the seven Tigrens chasing the little Carcalian had failed in their attempt to find the little wretch. Seven additional feet of height plus 500 pounds of muscle separated the two types of beings. Yet these seven Tigrens couldn't seem to catch this little fiend who had defiled their home turf! What's worse is that he made it to the village, and the seven of them would have to figure out a plan to deal with this failure. Either way, their existence would be revealed to those locals, and it would be over.

Chapter 2: BellBour Village

Shou 8, 5049

BellBour Village, a quaint little village by the Raoolen River is not far from Lake Leopold. The village had been a peaceful one, which has been around for five generations. The people of BellBour split off from the main city, Shalou, populated by nearly one-million Carcalians. The city is very active with industry and crime. Gangs of thieves roam the streets. They steal food from merchants, run off with beasts of burden, and rob those returning from their employers after receiving their week's pay. Rumor had it that a local crime syndicate had stolen baby Tigrens on route to Castle Shven-Shong in the hopes to harness their violent tendencies and turn them into soldiers. Unfortunately, when the Age of Shen-Long came, (the time when they first metamorphosize), the Tigrens didn't have the necessary training to focus their wild instincts. The seven of them supposedly ran off into the wilderness sixty years ago. Nobody really knows if it was true or not, the original families were killed when their babies were taken. The witnesses were never found and presumed dead. Any who could have helped were intimidated into submission.

The Crime Bosses in the Leonian Crime Syndicate coerce local businesses to pay them protection money so that their thugs

9

won't destroy their shops or kill them outright. They also divert supplies to their secret warehouses so they could sell the goods for a profit to fund their illegal activities. There were even rumors of several Crime agents that had infiltrated the Governor's Office, although that too was pure speculation.

It was because of this corruption that the founders of BellBour Village decided to split off from the city. They formed their own society based on cooperation and unity. Instead of buying goods with coins and pursuing a life to acquire wealth and status, BellBourians barter based on the value of goods or services. Meals are events held in the center of the village where everyone attends. The villagers have assigned tasks bent on the greater good of the village. There is a blacksmith guild, hospital guild, an agricultural guild, a hunter's guild, and a gatherer's guild, one for animal husbandry, one for builders, and an elected council to oversee the rules of the town and make important decisions. The council members elect new members every three years by popular vote. They nominate a governor, which takes control in emergencies.

A hospital guild was one of the first guilds formed, for life in the forest at first was very dangerous. Creatures, like the six-legged Tansor, live in the forest preying on unsuspecting Carcalians. Tansors are furry carnivorous predators that can stand upright, climb, and push over trees. They shoot a sticky

10

substance that immobilizes its prey like glue. Once absorbed through the skin, the substance causes the victim to go into a trance. Many Carcalians were injured by surprise attacks from these creatures.

Water is gathered from the Raoolen River through a dam and aqueduct system that feeds into a filtering system made of sand, charred wood, and paper. Wildlife in the water doesn't get into the aqueduct because of careful construction and rerouting. If by chance any aquatic animals get through, caretakers are there to make sure they are returned to the water before they die.

Crops are grown to supplement their diet of fruit, nuts, and small mammals. They raise larger animals to provide transportation and to haul heavy loads. They also use their meat as an alternate source of protein and their bones for jewelry, needles, weapon ornaments and handles, and building material. The entire animal is used, nothing goes to waste.

A very thick, reinforced stone wall to keep out animals protects the village. A moat filled with water diverted from the river encircles the village, preventing deadly water insects from breeding. Guards patrol the walls to make sure that criminals from Shalou City don't take advantage of the BellBourian hospitality. The drawbridge extends over the moat to let Carcalians into the village. The guards hold them in a debriefing room for a short period, to prove their authenticity and to prevent the harboring of criminals.

Schaintz, a blacksmith, was enjoying a cold mug of ale at the pub after a long day of working on a harness for the Babaloan family. After half an hour, he left the pub to return home for the evening. It had been a long day, and he was tired. On the way, he passed Todia, a shaklow breeder, who had been his friend most of his life. He waved and continued on his way.

Shaklows are bred for transportation, used to haul groups of Carcalians from place to place, and are often taken to neighboring villages for trade and breeding. They are four-legged and dark green, to blend in with the forest foliage. They stand six feet at the shoulder, and for a Carcalian of three feet, this is a big animal!

Schaintz turned a corner and noticed Shakeen, his mate from last year. He decided to just wave and continue on to his destination. Males are only allowed to see their pups on the 'Day of Taudee', which only occurs every 13 days after the pup has been weaned from the mother's milk. He arrived at home at the end of the street. His neighbors Bainser and TDow were caring for their lawns. He shouted a greeting to them both and went inside for a long recuperation. Bainser was a hunter, and every 26 days it would be his turn to go out hunting for small game. Bainser was the type to bring back two or three Tansors, which stand 12 feet high and are very dangerous. TDow was an expert at making weapons from metals traded from the big cities, which had the ability to mine the mountains for valuable minerals. He often works closely with Schaintz to make specialized weapons for Bainser, being that he was so fearless.

Night fell over the harmonious villagers, unaware of what approached from the east. A certain Carcalian had been camping in the northeast woods near Lake Leopold. The Tigrens ransacked his campsite, stole his food, and killed and ate his shaklow. He then hid in a nearby cave for the night, trying desperately to make his way to the village, hoping for sanctuary.

His name was Liotoch, and he had journeyed to these woods to get away from city life for a few days. The constant hustle and bustle of urban life was enough to drive anybody mad, let alone an abandoned cub like himself. He was only six, barely old enough to mate, and now he was running for his life.

He saw the village in the distance and began shouting:

"Open the drawbridge…, hurry…, I'm being chased… by a pack of wild Tigrens! Please…, hurry…, they're right behind me!" He shouted the words as best as he could, for he was running so fast and was almost completely out of breath.

The guards gave each other a puzzled look and granted their scared brother his wish. The drawbridge extended, Lio ran inside, and then the bridge retracted.

Chapter 3: Quest

Shou 8, 5049

The drawbridge lowered and the orange-red, out-of-breath Carcalian was certainly very shook-up about something, that was for sure.

"… and they hit me with this Felowitzer…" Lio huffed

"Felowitzer?" they exclaimed, "only the Tigrens use that and it's supposed to only be used during the Games. It's illegal to use outside the Weapons Tournament because it causes paralysis. It leaves a special type of mark…," said Zando.

"Check to see if he has the welt!" said Wenj.

A big red ring was visible in and amongst Lio's back hair, an unmistakable sign of the truth.

"Let's take him to the holding area, get him some yellato juice. Would you like that, kid?" said Zando.

"Okay, but what happens next? Those Tigrens were on my heels just as I ran in, what if they…"

"We'll worry about that. First we must speak with the Governor to determine a course of action."

"Blast, we lost him!! He's probably in there now, telling them to set fire to the forest to drive us out," said Teelor.

"Shut-up Teelor, or do you want everyone in Raoolia to know where we are?" scolded Fent.

"What's the plan Denzcan? They're bound to send a team out here to check out their story!" said Babbel.

"Everybody, hush up, or I'm going to stick my claws in to each and every one of your sorry hides!!" said Denzcan. "We'll wait and see what happens. If they send a search party, we'll deal with that," he said. "But mark my words, if you guys screw-up and get caught, I'll leave you to those rodents."

The two guards took Lio to a waiting room, with yellato juice and blam-bird tea waiting for him. It had seemed like forever since he'd had any blam-bird tea! The guards left to go to the governor, who lived near the center of town. Because it was getting dark, he'd be home, probably eating dinner by now. He'd know what to do!

They knocked at the door.

"Who's there? It had better be good if you're knocking at this hour!" He opened the door to see the second shift guards standing before him.

"What is it? Can't you see how late it is?"

"We're sorry sir, but we've encountered an unusual situation," said Zando.

"Well, spit it out, I haven't got all night!"

"Ye-es sir," he stammered.

He proceeded to tell the governor of the traveler that they encountered just at the end of shift change.

"And he had the welt from the Felowitzer? How odd! Hmm. Let me sleep on it. Decisions are best made not in haste. You are dismissed."

"Thank you, sir." With a salute, the guards were off to see that Lio had accommodations for the night. They then went to their respective homes for the night.

Shou 9, 5049

The next morning, having slept in a warm, comfortable bed for the night, Lio awoke and went into the kitchen to find a middle-aged Carcalian male roasting a piece of sqwich over a warm fire.

"Did you sleep well?" said Schaintz.

"Very well, thanks," he began, "It's nice to know that at any minute your life may be over!" he said sarcastically. "My name is Liotoch, but everyone calls me Lio."

"I'm Schaintz. I'm the local blacksmith. I make the hunting weapons around here. My neighbors help me out with various things. They loaned me the extra bed. So what brings you to our fair village?"

"Wild Tigrens."

A look of shock and confusion crossed Schaintz's face.

"Wild Tigrens? Ain't no such thing. They're all given to the Academies when they're born. Couldn't be. Maybe it was something else?"

"Hey," he said angrily, "I don't care what you say. I was almost killed by seven of them!"

"How'd ya know that they were wild Tigrens? Maybe you broke into the Academy and made them angry," he said, with a suspicious glance.

"They used a Felowitzer on me. Do trained Tigrens do that? No. They'd be able to take me before I could get ten feet from their school. Anyway, I was at Lake Leopold."

Schaintz continued to turn the spit as the sqwich roasted in the fireplace, not knowing how to respond to Lio's point.

The governor summoned the whole village to a town meeting. He had one of the assistance pass out fliers that read:

ON THIS DAY, 5049, SHOU 10

Meet all in the town square for an
Announcement from the governor,
Concerning the traveler.
All must attend – The Governor

Shou 10, 5049

The village gathered, as instructed, in the center of town, where the council would often announce their decrees to the villagers at a moment's notice.

"A great mystery is before us," he began, "a traveler comes from the east, near Lake Leopold with a disturbing story. Wild Tigrens are in our midst and are determined to take his life."

He paused as the murmur from the audience grew to a dull roar.

"Please, I need your attention. I need four brave volunteers to go out and search out these disturbing rumors. Who shall step forth?"

Schaintz, TDow, Todia, and Bainser stepped forth and said in unison: "We shall go."

"It is settled then. Go into the woods with the stranger, armed of course, and root out this mystery."

The five brave souls went to the workshop where weapons were made to prepare for combat. Swords and shields would need to be made, along with Felowitzer Shields to defend themselves from attack. There is much work to be done.

Schaintz began with the swords, hammering each one, and then sending it to TDow for mounting on the hilt and grip.

19

TDow would then return it to Schaintz for tempering, sharpening, and polishing. After enough swords were made for the five of them, he began work on the shields.

Meanwhile, Todia was preparing his strongest and fastest shaklows to catch the Tigrens, if they needed to run. Todia was also devising an entrapment system with the shaklows, using them to 'tighten the noose' if you will, on the *prey!*

Shou 16, 5049

When all was ready, the five brave Carcalians went to the drawbridge, to meet their destinies. Be it in victory or in death, they would not go down without giving it their all.

Chapter 4: Bait and Switch

Shou 16, 5049

The five heroes set forth into the forest to root out the evil that had blackened their lives. Their fear was as thick as a foggy night, yet they persevered, cutting their way through the grueling thoughts of eminent death.

"I don't believe it! _They're_ hunting us! Those puny, sad varmints actually think they have a shot against us!" said Puven.

"Never underestimate the will of your enemy, Puven. They could be much more dangerous than you think!" advised Denzcan.

"With what? A couple of swords and shields and a few Shaklows?" replied Puven.

"It isn't brute strength that wins the day, it's often brains, of which you lack a great deal!" remarked Babbel.

Puven unsheathed his claws, "We'll see what wins in the end!" Denzcan pulled out the Felowitzer and shot Puven in the back. He fell to the ground, unconscious.

"Tie him up. We'll use him as bait." Denzcan schemed.

"So, what's the plan," Lio said to Schaintz, "I mean they're seven feet taller and a hundred times stronger. How are we supposed to catch them, much less defeat them?"

"Todia, did you bring the rope as I asked?"

"Here ya go." he said, handing the rope to Schaintz.

"We're going to rig this up to the height of their necks, of which they'll fall backwards and we'll pounce!"

"*That's* your plan?" asked Lio with skepticism. "What if it doesn't work, we'll be dead," he mocked.

"Hey, just be happy you're getting any help. Besides, it won't work on all of them, I just need one. While that one is unconscious, TDow and Todia will allow themselves to be chased, leading them into a pit, which will keep the rest of them busy while we take that one prisoner. Then we'll take the captured Tigren back to the village as proof of their existence. As a back-up plan, we have our swords and shields to defend ourselves. Now come."

The five Carcalians set the trap as planned. While Schaintz and Lio were rigging up the rope, Todia, TDow and Bainser were digging a hole big enough to trap their adversaries.

With the hole dug, and the rope rigged, each took their positions. Schaintz banged the flat side of his sword on his shield to grab the Tigrens' attention.

Meanwhile, the six Tigrens had been watching and listening to their plan all along. Because Puven had been unconscious, they decided to sacrifice him. They untied the skeptic, and they all moved over to the bushes and trees where the pit was, concealed by leaf litter and branches. Puven awoke all alone, to the sound of metal hitting metal.

"There they are! Hey, where is everybody?" he said aloud. Puven decided that he didn't need the others to take care of this pitiful band of losers. He could take care of them all!

Just then, out of nowhere, one of the Tigrens sprung from the bushes, running full speed at the party! The five of them followed the plan and sure enough, Puven fell for the clothesline maneuver! Flat on his back, disoriented, and semi-conscious, the Carcalians tied him up. Two more Tigrens sprung from the bushes and chased Schaintz and TDow towards the pit. Just before they reached the pit, a Felowitzer bolt dropped the two Carcalians flat on their faces. Teelor and Sando bound the two so they couldn't move and returned to their hiding places.

"Well, I think this Tigren is good and secure. Let's meet up with the others. I heard them just ahead." said Todia.

"Help me rig him to the shaklows first. We'll take him with us." said Bainser.

The three arrived at the second trap only to find their companions tied up and the pit still concealed. They rushed over to untie them.

"What happened?" said Lio. "How did this happen?"

"I don't know, it's as if they…" began Schaintz.

Just then, six Tigrens appeared from every direction and before the five knew it, they were all hit with Felowitzers.

"Untie Puven, he looks pathetic in those ropes." said Denzcan.

After releasing Puven from his ropes, Fent said, "See, brute strength doesn't always win!"

Wensha smirked, but Puven was in no mood for jokes.

"Well at least *you* caught them," he grumbled.

"Yeah, we overheard their whole plan, and then pounced!"

At the confinement area, Denzcan was pondering what to do with his captives. Surely, the village will start looking for them once they've convinced themselves that the party had been gone too long. The best defense is a good offense, and the only way to stop them from invading these woods again will be to take control of the village.

The three missing Tigrens scanned the prisoners and reveled in their victory.

"Now what? We've got five varmints to deal with instead of one." said Puven.

"Just the Coug I wanted to see," said Denzcan. "Since you have been wronged by these 'varmints', then it will be your job to march them back to that cave we passed 60 strides back. Secure the entrance and meet us back here. I'm going to need all of you for the next task!"

Chapter 5: Consummation and Destruction

Shou 16, 5049

"Get going. I want to be rid of you as quickly as possible." said Puven. He kicked Bainser in the back, and as he fell forward, they all toppled like dominoes. They had had their hands tied together, ironically, by the same rope they had brought to capture the Tigrens.

"You must feel real good about yourself, kicking a little Carcalian in the back like that. You must make your mother proud!" squawked Bainser.

He picked Bainser up by the neck, raising the others up as well, and said, "Can it, varmint, or I'll squash you like the insect you are!" The rest of the journey went without incident. They soon arrived at the cave where Lio had hidden from the pursuing giants just days before. The five were sent into the cave, still tied together. Puven kicked and punched at the ceiling of the entrance until rocks came crashing down, sealing the entrance almost completely, except for a small air hole, too small for even the Carcalians to squeeze through.

"That should prolong your suffering and make your deaths that much more agonizing!" beamed Puven.

Arriving back at the camp that the other six Tigrens made, Puven had a glow about him that was not there when he left. It was no doubt because he received his retribution from the trip to the cave.

"Well it's about time, Puven, what were you doing, beating the feces out of them?" said Sando.

"Enough! I need everyone for this mission. I don't need any petty bickering!" interrupted Denzcan. "Now, here is what we're going to do."

Eyes widened, gasps came forth, and sinister smiles appeared as Denzcan told them of his plan. It was an ambitious goal, and if they survived, it would only be with The Luck of Pantherion, Granter and Keeper of the Fates. It was also what the fourth moon had been called, since its gravity tended to affect the other three moons, the rise and fall of the seas, and the length of the day. Yes, Pantherion would be with them, and victory over these small fries would be theirs!

"The first task is to get across the moat, so we need a raft. Teelor and Babbel, get to it. After we cross the moat, we'll need to get through the wall. Fent and Sando, go out and collect some baklovites. They can tunnel through anything! Puven, Wensha, and I will be making firebombs. This village burns tonight! Does everyone have their Felowitzers?" asked Denzcan.

"Yeah, yes, yup, got mine, uh yeah, yep," they all said.

"Good. When we set fire to the village, hit the fleeing Carcalians with your Felowitzers. We'll round 'em up and begin my *Master Plan*!" schemed Denzcan.

Night fell over the slumbering residents of BellBour. There was a full Tigerion tonight, a crescent Leonada, a half Cheetahn, and a New Pantherion. Perfect. The Fates are with them tonight. This victory would cement Denzcan as an effective leader and would pave the way to a possible power struggle, if not carefully held.

The five heroes had gone out early yesterday, and still hadn't returned. There was an uneasy feeling in the village. They should have been back by now. I mean, if they hadn't found anything, they would have been back at nightfall. The silence was an uneasy, paranoid silence, one that occurs before a cataclysmic eruption, or a rockslide, or...

"Fire! The main house of the Governor is on fire! Get the water buckets! Drag the feeding troughs over, so we can form a brigade! Get water from the central fountain if you have to!"

Balls of fire rained down on the village, when one fire was under control, five more appeared, seemingly from the Gods themselves. But why would the Gods rain fire down upon us? Everyone scattered, trying to find a safe place, which ended up being the village square. Whoever or whatever had done this had deliberately targeted the buildings, as if it had been planned!

Suddenly, Carcalians started dropping like flies! Before we could all scatter, faces and dirt were married. In minutes, the Felowitzers had subdued us with its overwhelming influence. Seven Tigrens approached and tied our hands together. When the affects of the blast had worn off, we were marched out of the village, through the drawbridge, over the moat, and into the forest. Our fate would surely be grim! Our village was on fire, our security shattered, and our spirits were heavy in our souls.

Shou 17, 5049

The train of Carcalian prisoners arrived at the cave site, where Lio had begun his quest for help, and where once he had been free, now was held captive. The boulders were removed one by one by those thundering beasts, the Tigrens, and the fresh air on our faces felt really good. When the boulders were finally cleared, thirty males, fifteen females, and forty yearlings, no doubt from the village, were all piled into the cave, which became tinier by the minute. What would they do with us? Will we all die at the hands of these merciless beasts, or was there some other plan in store for us?

Felowitzer bolts then were shot at us all. We slammed into each other, into walls, onto dirt.

"Puven, Wensha, Babbel, gather up all the old-timers, we've got no use for them. Teelor, Fent, Sando, and I will keep an eye out for any movement. Keep your weapons at the ready."

The older Cougrans were rounded up into a pile. When the affects of the Felowitzer had worn off, each was killed by hand by the captors, for all the females and yearlings to see. The trauma was nearly unbearable for the adults; the yearlings must have been absolutely horrified!

"You all work for me now. I *own* you! If any of you refuse to do as you are told, you will be killed. I have a project that needs to be done, and many hands make a big job seem small," amused Denzcan. Turning to his six-pack members, he said, "Seal the prisoners in the cave. We will begin work when a site is found."

Book 2: The Journey to Shven-Shong

Chapter List:

Chapter 6:   Discovery..   32

Chapter 7:   Hierarchy..   37

Chapter 8:   On the Move..   45

Chapter 9:   Power...   51

Chapter 10:   Manipulation..   57

Chapter 6: Discovery

Shou 17, 5049

"Shalou is a nice place to visit and trade, but I wouldn't want to live there," said Zampdom. "It's unfortunate that we can only get Cougrinium from the city."

"Well if the mountains of Nidia weren't half way around the world, we wouldn't need to go there," said Yelilah. "Besides, how are we supposed to make bits and harnesses without that metal? Why, whatever would poor Schaintz do if he didn't have Cougrinium?" she said with a smile.

Zampdom and Yelilah had been the trading liaisons since they had turned 15, two years ago. Since their mating cycles were over, the male and female were free to fraternize. Male and female Carcalians less than 15 do not have jobs together, unless they are father and daughter, and it would be before the daughter's first mating cycle.

BellBour was shrouded in the trees, and so they didn't notice that it lay in charred ruin, but they could smell it!

"Do you smell that?" asked Yelilah.

"Yeah, I do. What do think it is?" replied Zampdom.

"It smells like something got burned" responded Yelilah.

32

"We'd better hurry back to the village. I'm sure the Council will want to hear about this!" said Zampdom. "It might be a forest fire! But started by what, or who?"

"Let's not speculate," replied Yelilah.

They arrived at what used to be BellBour Village, and all they saw was charred homes, a thin, smoky mist, and the absence of all the inhabitants!

"What is going on? Where is everybody?" asked Yelilah.

"I don't know, but it doesn't look good. Look at how disturbed the dirt is! It looks like everyone gathered here. And look at those huge tracks! Only a Tigren has feet that big!" said Zampdom.

"But Tigrens don't bother with us. I wonder what could have happened." Yelilah said, in a bewildered tone.

"Let's follow the tracks and see where they lead," suggested Zampdom.

"Good idea," agreed Yelilah.

A short distance ahead...

"Look, now all the tracks are in single file!" Yelilah said, pointing about. "That's not good."

"No, so let's stick to the bushes for cover. I have no doubt that the situation is a dangerous one. It's likely that the

Council is no longer in charge. We must alert the Shven-Shong. They'll be able to handle this," suggested Zampdom.

"Not yet. We don't have anything to tell them. We need to give them the location of these fiends."

"Alright, we'll do it your way." agreed Zampdom.

They followed the tracks until they overheard someone talking.

"I have a project that needs to be done and many hands make a big job seem small. Seal the prisoners in the cave. We will begin work when a site is found."

"I think we found out what happened to our village, but why are they being held?" wondered Zampdom aloud.

"We've found out where they are, now let's go!" urged Yelilah. "The Shven-Shong's Castle is so far from here, if we want to make it there before they all die, we'd better get going!"

"We're gonna have to find a quicker way than on foot. C'mon, I've got an idea." Zampdom said with a mischievous smile.

"I think we should camp for the night," said Yelilah, "we can't do anything until morning anyway."

Shou 18, 5049

The next morning they departed from the prison encampment and headed east toward the ruins of BellBour. Zampdom was gazing skyward every few minutes, up into the canopy. He was looking for a particular animal to take them to the edge of the continent, where the castle is located. Zampdom smiled when he found what he was looking for.

"Look, there's our ride. No harness to keep us on though, so we'll have to improvise." schemed Zampdom.

"I'm not riding one of those pekalls without a harness. I could be killed, maimed, or worse." worried Yelilah.

"Do you have a better idea?"

"No… but… I don't like this one!" she hissed.

"Here, take my extra knife and cut some vines twice your height. I learned how to make a make-shift harness and saddle some years back," he instructed.

When the saddles and harnesses were made, they set out to catch themselves two pekalls in order to get to the Shven-Shong Academy in their lifetime. What they didn't know was a certain Tigren had tracked them and decided that now was the time to make his move!

Out of the bushes leapt one of the Tigrens that they had seen at the prison encampment several hours ago. He grabbed Yelilah's foot, just as the two aged Carcalians leapt in different directions. Yelilah fell head first into the dirt and got a mouthful for her efforts to flee. Zampdom, when he saw the Tigren grab Yelilah, doubled back and jumped on the attacker's back. He wrapped his arm around his neck and began choking the blood supply to his brain. When the Tigren had lost consciousness, the two clamored up the nearest Grantahn tree, where pekalls were known to roost.

Pekalls are relatively docile and easy to catch, just as long as you are very quiet and don't spook them. Two were sighted by the fleeing villagers. They leapt onto the pekalls' back and fitted their homemade harnesses over the winged creatures' faces! Pekalls have a 20-foot wingspan and are 8 feet in length from nose to tail. Their heads are almond shaped and they have flat teeth for grinding the plants that they eat in the trees. With a snap of the vines, the two were off to the Shven-Shong Academy, located on the northeastern tip of Raoolia. With their journey to the ends of Raoolia underway, a moment of peace enters their minds, maybe for just a brief moment...

Chapter 7: Hierarchy

Shou 18, 5049

Puven awoke several minutes later, only to see his prey depart to the west. There was no doubt they were going to inform the Shven-Shong of what they had overheard, the exact details of which remains unclear. He decided to go back and tell Denzcan so that a plan made to deal with this crisis.

"Where did Puven go in such a blasted hurry?" asked Fent.

"No doubt on some crazy chase like always," replied Wensha.

"What do you think he saw?" wondered Fent.

Just then, Puven appeared, seemingly from nowhere. Speak of The Evil One, and he appears.

"I caught two Carcalians spying on our little gathering. They commandeered a couple of pekalls and headed northwest toward Castle Shven-Shong."

Denzcan came forward, with a suspicious glare, he asked, "How did they escape? You're ten feet tall! They're three feet, what happened?"

37

"They were fully matured, and I took them by surprise, but the male got behind me and choked me. I guess I passed out," he replied, embarrassed and disappointed.

"Well that's the second foul-up in two days, Puven. You're about as useful as a shaklow with a broken leg," he sneered. "I've got a plan to move the prisoners anyway. This time, we'll cover our tracks. That was and is your job Puven, so make sure it gets done right!" Denzcan turned for a moment, then turned back, "Oh yeah, I almost forgot..." Denzcan unsheathed his claws and swiped at Puven, leaving five deep wounds in his chest. "If you ever fail again, I will kill you slowly. Babbel, Wensha, dress his wounds so he scars. I want you all to remember this day. You will pay the price for failing me!"

Teelor and Sando were assigned scout duty to find a new location big enough to house the new prisoners and a place not obvious to the Shven-Shong Clan.

"I wish I knew the whole plan. Just getting bits and pieces here and there is unnerving," said Sando. "I mean, we're all pack-mates. We can be trusted, right?"

"I think there is something more going on here than what Denzcan is telling us. He seems to be holding back something, but what?" said Teelor.

"Well, what do we know? He wants us to scout out a long-term place to house his prisoners. He has this *big plan* that he's not sharing with us. I wonder if it has to do with that rock he saw last week, you know, the one that fell from the sky. Ever since then it's been, 'I'm the leader' and 'Do this' and now it's 'You'll pay the price for failure'. What is going on?" Sando shouted, in frustration.

"All I know is that Puven is going to be history if we don't do something. He screws-up all the time! He's a joke! Why would Denz even waste his time?" Teelor thought aloud. "It just doesn't make sense."

"I agree with you. Maybe we have to work a little treachery of our own to get to the bottom of this," mused Sando. "But first, let's go find a spot. Denz mustn't know our plans until it's too late!"

"Ah, subterfuge, I like it!" schemed Teelor.

Teelor and Sando made their way east, following the river towards Lake Leopold. They would have to cross the river, west of the lake, to find enough land to house all of those Carcalians. They've never seen the forest north of the lake, for they crossed the Raoolen in the west, when they escaped from Shalou City. They concluded, after walking several hours that it might be better to move off the continent. But moving several hundred

Carcalians over the Straits of Raoolia might bring unwanted attention from the Ringlue and Shven-Shong Clans.

"The Straits of Raoolia are narrow; we could very well go to Sphynxia. The Ringlue Clan is much smaller than the Shven-Shong. We could remain hidden there until such time when we can reveal ourselves," suggested Sando.

"Let's run this by Denz," said Teelor, "so that he can take full credit for the idea. He wouldn't want one of us peons to actually come up with an idea, or anything!" he remarked, with a thick dose of sarcasm. They camped for the night and decided to return in the morning.

Meanwhile, back at base camp, Denzcan was deep in thought while waiting for his two scouts to return.

'I'll use these Carcalians to build a massive Temple, bigger than anything ever built,' Denzcan thought. 'A temple needs a God to rule over it, and that God shall be me! That rock that fell from the sky south of here shall be my next task. Since this distraction with the Carcalians is taken care of, I now have a chance to go and get it! I need a second in command to take care of things while I'm away. But who? Puven is definitely not a candidate. Sando, Teelor, and Babbel are less worthy, although capable. Perhaps it will be Fent.'

"Fent, come here," said Denzcan.

"Yeah?" he replied.

"I need to go out for a bit. Can you handle things while I'm away?" asked Denzcan.

"What do you need me to do, we're just sitting here."

"Make sure the slaves are fed, send out Wensha and Babbel. Keep an eye out for Puven, wherever he is. He's bound to do something stupid. When Teelor and Sando come back, have them just hang out until I come back. Got it?" asked Denzcan.

"Yeah, I got it," replied Fent.

Denzcan went south; in the direction where he thought the meteorite had slammed into the ground. He estimated that it was a three-day trek to the crash site. The rock almost called to him, pulling him toward it as if it was his fate to find the lost rock. The 'pull' continued as the first and second days ended. By the third day, he knew the exact location and he arrived at sundown.

Shou 20, 5049

Teelor and Sando returned to the camp from their scouting expedition in northern Raoolia to await further instructions from their self-crowned leader.

Shou 21, 5049

The rock was approximately three feet in diameter. It came to rest after digging a trench in the ground in a clearing in the forest. The heat alone that it had radiated after impact had wilted some of the surrounding plants. But because it had cooled for several days, it was easy to chisel off a sliver. It cleaved rather easily into a disc-shaped piece. He gazed at the beautiful red and blue marbling of the rock. It glowed a light blue in his hand as a mist slowly slithered through the air toward him. Denzcan was mesmerized by its beauty, drinking in its power...its *majesty*...its **glory**!

After several minutes, he broke from the trance and decided to return to the camp. He fastened it to a belt he had made several days ago, which he kept hidden from the other Tigrens during the distraction with the Carcalians. He clipped the belt around his waist.

Suddenly, he was lifted off the ground, and he could feel a surge of sheer power run through his body like lightening through a metal pole! A blinding light flashed from his floating body in all directions! He radiated so much heat that the forest was set on fire 500 strides in every direction! He had a passing thought that he had wished the fire had never started, and the forest returned to normal! Denzcan decided to return to camp using his newfound power. He flew most of the way back and landed half a day's walk from the campsite. He walked the rest of the way and none of the others were wise to their leader's newfound powers.

Shou 22, 5049

"Gather around fellow Tigrens. I come to you with an announcement. There will now be a hierarchy amongst our pack. I am your new RRandoll, Fent is my RRan, Sando and Teelor are the scouts, Wensha, Babbel, and Puven are Slavers. Does anyone here oppose this ranking?" announced the new Emperor Denzcan.

"We do!" said Teelor and Sando in unison. They ran at the new Emperor and were suddenly on their backs, as if they had ran into a wall. They suddenly began to float above the ground, upside-down! The new Emperor walked over to the two treacherous attackers.

"If you wish to live, you will obey me," said the RRandoll. *"You shall have the honor of calling me Master RRandoll. In fact, I am Master RRandoll to you all! This is what will happen if you don't."*

Just then, Teelor and Sando went flying into a tree. They crashed to the ground like rocks from the sky.

"So I say again, does anyone oppose?" Silence was their only answer. *"Then kneel before your GOD!"* As he looked around, all the Tigrens knelt and nothing but utter fear

could be seen in their eyes, giving credence to his newfound authority!

Chapter 8: On the Move

Shou 18, 5049

"Flying… is the only way to travel," said Yelilah with a stretch and a yawn. "I never knew pekalls were such steady fliers!"

"This beats walking any day! You see...nothing to worry about! This should cut our travel time down from a month to two days!" replied Zampdom.

"It's too bad pekalls are day fliers and not able to see at night or we could be there by tomorrow. I'm sure our comrades from the village will want a quick end to their stay at the cave," she commented. "What do you think will happen when that Tigren wakes up and tells the others that we got away with this vital information?" she asked.

"Well, there are only two choices. One, they could come after us, which is unlikely, or two, they can run. If that's the case, then all of the Clans need to be alerted. If they cross the Straits of Raoonada to Cougranada and hide in the forests around the abandoned castles, we'll never find them!"

"Sphynxia...," began Yelilah, "Sphynxia is the most likely choice. It's closer, warmer, and it's easier to feed all those new members they have now added to their pack."

"True," replied Zampdom.

They glided northwest, in the direction of hope, and landed on the other side of Shalou City, half way to their destination. They built a fire and camped for the night.

The wilderness of Raoolia was teeming with life. Night, it seemed, was a popular time for the animals to come out. There are Tonias that shout their calls all night long. Zampdom and Yelilah often had sleepless nights in heavily populated Tonia country. Tonias are little mammalian creatures that have four legs, wings, long prehensile tails, and opposable thumbs. They tend to live in family groups of twenty or so, and are a staple of BellBourian diets, when Tansor meat could not be found.

The fire crackled under the fresh Tonia sizzling over the flames. Zampdom went up the Tanwanna Tree, where they like to nest for the night, and was able to spear one. He had learned to hunt in the two years he and Yelilah had journeyed back and forth to Shalou City. There were also a couple of Bengal fruits boiling on the hot rocks, so their skins, which were bitter, could be removed. The two tired travelers ate their meal and slept until the bright blue dawn wrestled them from the land of slumber.

Shou 19, 5049

The next morning the two mounted up and soared off, now crossing the beach and harbor of Raoolia. The Academy is on the northern-most tip, right across the water from the Ringlue

Clan's Academy. They arrived on schedule and glided into a clearing near the gate entrance.

"Who enters the domain of the Shven-Shong? State your purpose here." commanded the guard. The world seemed to shake as he spoke the words. Obviously, he is a ten-foot Tigren, but a world of difference existed between the wild and the trained. This one has a commanding presence that was obviously absent from the foes that they had encountered.

"The only two remaining BellBourians that escaped the clutches of enslavement by a pack of wild Tigrens," he replied. "I am Zampdom and she is Yelilah."

"What do you mean *enslavement* by *wild Tigrens*?" he growled.

"A pack of Tigrens burned our village to the ground and took all of our people captive. We were in Shalou City when it happened. Will you help us?" asked Yelilah in a blur.

The Guard snarled. "A pack, you say? Hmmm..." 'There were rumors, but no proof that a pack existed. Perhaps others know more,' the guard thought. "I will let you pass after I've consulted with my Shandowl."

The two travelers waited several hours for the guard to return. At sunset, the drawbridge lowered and the guard ushered them in.

Inside the Tigren's Den, the Academy was a huge stone building with multiple levels, both above and below ground. Their walls were covered with massive tapestries, and their torches burned in stone basins. They walked down one floor, and entered a cylindrical tower. They stepped on the platform and the guard pulled a rope, and all of a sudden, the three Cougrans were moving upward at a high rate of speed! The platform stopped abruptly, almost as suddenly as it began. They stepped over the crevasse that separated the platform and the floor. The two newcomers were asked to sit at a rectangular table. A red-robed figure with a chain-claw (Shven-Shong) crown was waiting at the head of the table.

"I am Shandowl Raulian," he said. His speaking voice was more like a roar that rattled the air and ground around the diminutive Carcalians. "I am told that a wild pack has enslaved your people. How many in this pack?" he asked.

"There are seven. One would be easy to take care of, and we wouldn't have bothered, but the two of us can't overcome seven of them," said Zampdom.

"Then it is true," said the Shandowl.

"May I ask, what is true, mighty Shandowl?" asked Yelilah.

"About 60 years ago, a criminal syndicate called The Leonians tried to raise an army of Tigrens, but failed. Their initial capture, to see if it was even possible, was seven. Those seven fled after the Age of Shen Long, the age where Tigrens first metamorphosize. We investigated, but there weren't any witnesses. We believe but cannot prove that the crime syndicate had intimidated everyone to the point of looking the other way. So without any witnesses or evidence, we could only document it as a rumor," answered Raulian. "Now that we know of you two witnesses, we can begin looking for these *wild* ones and deal with them."

"We believe that they will move, if they haven't already. The leader mentioned a large project that he had in mind for our people," mentioned Zampdom.

"Yes…yes of course." replied Raulian, who was now deep in thought. He turned to the guard that was standing behind Zampdom. "Get a squad of twelve together to hunt these treacherous fiends down! Make sure to tell them that the Carcalians are not to be hurt, especially if they use them as shields. NOW!!!" he roared.

"Yes sire," the guard said, almost trembling.

Shou 21, 5049

After two days, a squad of the twelve best warriors was assembled by the guard for this important mission: two trackers, four weapons experts, four hand-to-hand combat experts, and two snipers. The crew of twelve mounted up on their dragons, and the two Carcalians mounted up on their pekalls. The dragons were of serpentine origin, and could fly and swim quite easily. On the ground, with their wings folded, the dragons crawled on their bellies, twisting and turning to navigate any terrain.

Shou 22, 5049

The rescue party flew at the pekall's pace by day, and slept on the dragons' backs while they slithered on the ground by night. Serpentine dragons rarely sleep, and are perfectly suited for long distance traveling. They reached the cave in a day and a half, but found nothing. The trackers were sent out to pick up the Wild Tigrens' trail. The rest of the group made camp, for nothing could be done until they returned.

Chapter 9: Power

Shou 22, 5049

The six other Tigrens weren't sure what to think. Denzcan was no more, now there was this weirdo named Master RRandoll. He was obviously very powerful, and dethroning him would not be attempted by the wise. No, they were stuck in this predicament and there would be no getting out.

"It's time to move," said Master RRandoll, **"Teelor and Sando, if you are done being treacherous, lead the way to the location you found. Sphynxia, right?"**

"That's right," said Teelor, "how did you know?"

"I know all things. Now, go forth and I shall meet you when you arrive. My pet will accompany you on your journey."

Out of thin air appeared a four-legged, winged drakell, one like the populations found in the mountains of Felinia. Drakells were large reptiles that made their homes in the mountains and came to the valleys and forests to feed on large prey. He was forty feet tall and eighty feet long, brown, and had a spiked tail.

"Rrondoxia will keep you company, won't you?"

"I'll keep my best eye on them. Ha, ha, ha, ha, ha, haaa!" it laughed.

All gasped at the talking drakell. That meant no deception could take place, no planning of treacherous deeds either.

"I will see you in three days time, at the northern coast. Since amateur trackers weren't deceived by your methods, Puven, I will take care of the covering of tracks. The Shven-Shong are quite formidable," said Master RRandoll.

The party shoved off, all the remaining Carcalians, the drakell, and the six Tigrens began their journey to the coast. That meant non-stop walking all day long, crossing the Raoolen River, and trudging through the forest to the northern shore of Raoolia.

The new super being flew to the south, back toward the rock that afforded him such power. He reached it in less than an hour, flying faster than he had the previous day. After retrieving the meteorite, he used his mind to levitate the rock below him as he flew. He knew that he would have to protect it so that he could remain unopposed. Being in such close proximity to the entire meteorite, his power, his awareness, and his knowledge of how to use this power increased ten times! He suddenly was able to sense the two travelers' movements through the air particles that had spied on him. Time seemed to become irrelevant and he began to see a barrage of images in his head, the past vision of the spies, the present flying through the air, and the future. All these images overwhelmed him and he fell out of the sky, like the meteorite, and hit the ground with a monstrous crash!

The sun had set, and it was night. Awakened by crawling insects, RRandoll sat upright, his head spinning. The power, the knowledge of the use of his magic all downloaded into his mind at once, was too much for him to handle. When he gained his composure, RRandoll began his search for the meteorite. He must keep it from all others so that only he could harness its power! Even though he had all the knowledge in his mind of how to use this newfound power, he knew that he would have to practice before he could master its secrets!

Master RRandoll stood-up and turned in the direction of the power rock. He flew to where it was located, and brought forth a box made of Cougrinium big enough to house the rock. He knew somehow that Cougrinium could block the effects of the stone enough for transport. The material wasn't a one-hundred percent block, but it reduced the overwhelming effects. With his telekinetic powers, he lifted the stone into the box and sealed it inside.

Sphynxia lay far to the north. Instinctively, he thought about how much easier it would be if he could instantly be where he wanted. Concentrating on the location, he, and the box, dematerialized from the crash site. Because he was thinking of the cave site, he rematerialized right where he remembered. *'I wonder what would happen if I concentrated on an object?'* he thought. He concentrated on destroying a rock. Nothing happened.

"Hmmm..."

As Master RRandoll was off on his own adventure and the drakell was leading the group of Tigrens with the slaves, Puven decided that he was not going to follow this path. He was going to go off on his own adventure, because he was certain that staying in this group was going to get him killed. It was easy because night had fallen. When the time was right, he began slipping backward in line, bending over to pick things up that he dropped, until finally he was the last one. When he was sure nobody was looking, he slipped into the bushes, waited for the team to move far enough ahead so he wouldn't be detected. He decided to head east, toward the eastern shore. A place where most don't go because of the huge predators that roam the beach, searching for beached sea creatures.

The group stopped for the night. Fent had suggested a head-count be done and that's when he noticed that there were only *four* other Tigrens! Puven was missing! Oh no! The last time he had seen Puven he was walking with Wensha and Babbel! Puven must have broken off somewhere along the way!

Then Rrondoxia sensed panic and fear in Fent. He walked over, and in a deep, resonating voice that permeated Fent's entire body, he said, "Why are you so *nervous*, Fent? Tell me or I'll squash you like the insect you are!"

"Uh, nothing…nothing to be concerned about!!" Fent began to shake.

"Nothing?" asked the drakell. "Then why are you trembling like a cornered cub?"

"Because… uh…"

Fire shot out of the drakell's nose, "Tell me or die!"

"Puven has left the group… sir…" a shaking Fent replied.

"Stay here," ordered the drakell. He spread his wings, leapt into the air, and just as quick as an arrow finding its mark, the giant beast was in the air and heading towards the sea. Since Master RRandoll was to the south, and the Shven-Shong were to the west, the only place for the coward to run was east.

After a day of flying, the drakell found his prey! The coward was running through the brush, as if he could get away from the mighty Rrondoxia! Not only could he see perfect detail, but he also had a special lens that allowed him to detect heat! He saw the fleeing coward below and began his descent toward his quarry. He sent out of a barrage of flames to encircle the

55

escapee. With a second swoop, he snatched up the coward out of the center and flew back to the group. When Master RRandoll finds out, there will be Hell to Pay!

Chapter 10: Manipulation

Shou 22, 5049

Raecholl and Sandewl were two of the twelve Tigrens that had been sent as part of the search party to discover what had happened to the BellBourians at the hands of the Wild Tigrens. They were highly trained trackers that could easily follow the most difficult trail left by the most elusive assailant.

"You take the northern quadrant and I'll take the eastern quadrant. It's unlikely that the group would go south. Cougranada is on the other side of some rough seas," stated Raecholl.

"Remember, we are to report back as soon as we find them. Do not engage, whatever happens," added Sandewl. Sandewl headed north, looking for the trail that would lead them to the prisoners. He searched for broken limbs, footprints, anything left behind.

Raecholl, heading east, stumbled upon a lone Tigren, running for dear life, due east. All of a sudden, fire shot out of the air and formed a circle around the running creature. Raecholl concealed herself in the brush. The next moment occurred faster than she could perceive. A rush of air and a pair of flopping wings passed right over her head, picked up the fleeing Tigren, and was gone! She caught sight of its direction just before it disappeared out of sight! Hopefully, Sandewl did not happen upon such a creature, even though it was heading in his direction! "I'd better find him," she muttered aloud.

In the distance, Sandewl could hear voices coming from above, and *then*...he saw *it*! When he was able to focus on the creature, he noticed it was carrying something! The drakell, usually not found in this part of the world, was carrying a *Tigren!* The captive was shouting something at the beast, but the beast was not reacting, it just kept flying north. Sandewl lost sight of the creature, just as his partner arrived.

"Did you get a fix on his heading?" Raecholl asked.

"Due north, heading towards the shore. I'm sure that creature has to be connected to these Wild Ones. But how?"

"It's not for us to know at this time. Come. We must report back to the team so we can mount our assault!"

"You fool! You've risked revealing our position, and for what, to bring back this coward?" scolded Babbel. The Rrondoxia whipped his tail around and swiped Babble off his feet.

"I am an extension of your Master, and if you wish to not become my next meal, I suggest you shut-up!" growled the drakell. He placed his left-front foot on Babbel, pinning him to the ground.

"Do you think this bickering is wise, drakell?" asked Fent. "After all, we should keep moving. We've rested long enough."

"Very well. We keep moving! Master RRandoll will be very upset if we are late!" replied Rrondoxia.

Flying high in to the clouds to avoid detection, Master RRandoll flew north. He could sense trouble with Puven, but he knew that his drakell had the team under control. An image in his mind formed, a spectacular step trapezoidal temple, right in the middle of Sphynxia. A glorious tribute to his power! He would not need the slaves to build it, but he would make use of them anyway.

Arriving at his destination quickly, RRandoll landed at the exact spot where the temple would be. After setting the Cougrinium box down, he opened it, unleashing the meteorite's full force! He would need every ounce of power to accomplish this feat!

The ground shook, like no other force could shake it! A small break in the dirt became a monstrous upheaval of rock! A crevasse ten miles long opened before the super-being! It began to spread in width and stopped at the ten-mile mark so that there was a huge, ten square mile hole in the ground. Rock began flying out of the great chasm forming a perimeter around it.

When enough rock had been removed for the temple, the ground closed, bringing the crevasse together as quickly and easily as it had opened.

Taking the meteorite in his hands, RRandoll concentrated on the rocks, increasing their temperature so he could fuse their molecules into individual squared off stones that were perfect cubes. When this was accomplished, he stacked them in six layers. The first layer had 13,000 stones by 13,000 stones, which were 39 feet square, covering approximately 96 miles! The second layer had 10,000 stones by 10,000 stones. The third layer had 7,000 by 7,000 stones, the forth layer had 4,000 by 4,000 stones, the fifth layer had 1,000 by 1,000 stones, the sixth had 700 by 700 stones, and the final layer had 400 by 400 stones. All of the stones were fused together at the molecular level into one piece of solid rock! Even though the temple was 96 miles square, it only reached a height of 234 feet, for each layer consisted only of one block.

In the top layer, the entrance was dissolved. Each layer had a series of mazes and was connected by a single set of stairs. This was to ensure that he'd be protected from any outsiders. On the bottom four levels, he created statues of sphinxes, all having huge empty sockets for eyes.

Because the temple was so huge, RRandoll feared that it would be found quite easily. The only solution would be to sink

mmW spectrum for true 5G can be deployed. There are enormous complexities to interworking and reconciling these dissimilar and competing networks and standards, which are anticipated to be pre-5G propositions. No one should stake a long-term, publicly funded commitment on them until after 2020, when mmW bands and devices that can handle them begin to become ubiquitously and globally standardized and licensed, with channels auto-managed among users in the case of shared-use spectrum and generally available for genuine 5G.

Reducing the number of users per cell. The last means of increasing capacity for an entire system is by reducing the number of users per cell. This is accomplished by placing cells closer and closer together so the same capacity once afforded to a large coverage footprint of one cell utilizing

overlaps must be planned carefully to minimize interference to neighboring cells so they can maintain capacity. Placing cells closer together requires reducing signal power by lowering transmitter powers, lowering antenna elevations, and/or tilting antennas radically downward. Any of these strategies forces the cells to be much smaller, shrinking their capacity footprints correspondingly.

In a 5G network, the resulting small cells indeed will need to be quite small. Moving cells closer together is especially difficult if a provider uses currently available sub-6 GHz spectrum that propagates too well for dense small-cell applications. Designs that meet the 5G bandwidth targets and accommodate future mmW ranges have made their coverage areas typically less than 1,000 feet in diameter – often half of this – and placed antennas only about 20 feet off the ground, with

of around 15 percent, this falls to around 1.5 Gbps of likely actual usable throughput available per cell, shared among all users.

This bandwidth, even shared, might seem like a lot compared with today's typical broadband speed of around 41 Mbps. But again, it is reasonable to expect median wireline broadband speed to approach 100–150 Mbps by 2020 and 1 Gbps by the 5G equipment end of life. In addition, wireline providers, particularly FTTP providers, typically do not have to limit monthly usage to avoid oversubscribing their shared broadband resources.

Today, IP video drives wireless providers to limit oversubscription of shared broadband resources. IP video is critical for distance learning, telemedicine, entertainment and other purposes. In days when bursty web-browsing traffic dominated the

the temple to its top level, and grow the jungle back with the displaced area. Master RRandoll then broke the meteorite into 8 pieces, molded them into spheres, and moved them to the four sphinx statues in the temple. The jungle would conceal his temple from those Academic Tigrens, and the mazes would protect the meteorite from being found. From this day forth, the meteorite will be known as The Eyes of the Four Sphynxes! He sunk the temple below the ground so that its top layer was the only part of the temple visible. He then flew off to meet his troop.

The stealthy trackers ran at full speed toward the cave site. Even at this hurried pace, they scarcely made a sound. They had been trained from an early age to track the most elusive of creatures in the forest, at different paces. To the shock of the rescue party, the trackers were on top of them before anyone heard a sound!

"We've…located the…direction they are…heading…" huffed Raecholl, "…due north."

"Then we must move now! Mount-up, we must reach them quickly and by surprise. Everyone, take to the air, we must go at top speed." ordered Svence.

Master RRandoll landed near the moving troop that was heading toward the north shore of Raoolia.

"Master, we didn't expect to see you so soon, what has happened?" asked Fent.

"Our trajectory has been revealed. The Shven-Shong approach," he snarled. *"I suspect that we have a deserter to deal with."* Master RRandoll looked at Puven. *"You have disgraced this pack once again; death would be too good for you!"*

Puven laughed off the remark. Just then, Master RRandoll pointed his finger at Puven and he began to change! Suddenly his upper body grew thick, long, brown fir. Horns grew out of his head, and his muzzle elongated. His feet turned into hoofs, his muscle tone increased, and his body changed into an upright primate. His mind changed also, and his only desire became the will to fight. A sword materialized for the creature, and he bowed before his master. Master RRandoll made the other five Tigrens into the same beast.

"His punishment shall be yours as well! I shall call your species Minotaur! You shall be immortal, and any limb removed will be regrown as new! Any damage incurred will heal as quickly as it was inflicted!" instructed Master RRandoll. *"Kneel before me my Minotaurs! Now go forth and battle the Shven-*

Shong! Take no prisoners, drive them off, or destroy them all!!"

While the Minotaurs marched south, Master RRandoll immobilized all the slaves into stone statues. He levitated the slaves, and flew toward the temple, with all 70 of them floating behind him. When he arrived, he placed all the slaves in their standing positions and turned each of them into 10-foot tall sphinxes. Each Sphynx was given the instinct to protect the temple and Master RRandoll's existence.

"Rrondoxia, through this portal you will go, into the spiritual realm, for you will be tasked to harvest the souls I will need to further my conquest of this world!" The drakell bowed, saying nothing, and walked through the portal that lay before him. His purpose would be revealed when needed, not now, but in the future...

Master RRandoll could manipulate matter at the atomic level, fusing the molecules together into rock, as well as manipulating living genetic material. He could rearrange genetic proteins with a thought, taught to him by The Great Eyes of the Four Sphynxes! He could fly because he could create a magnetic field opposite to the planet Cougran, which lifted him off the ground and he pulled himself through the air. He could also project this magnetic field around objects, levitating them off the ground! He could even gather atoms from the environment, change their atomic structures, or create them from thin air! That is how he was able to give his Minotaurs swords!

Shou 23, 5049

The Minotaurs marched south. The Shven-Shong flew north. The battle began with the first sighting of the Minotaur Army from the air. The dragons swooped down to land before the marching creatures, to ask if they had seen the Wild Tigrens.

"Attack!!" said one of the Minotaurs.

A dragon was speared with a sword. Metal clashed with metal as the battle ensued. The trackers were hacked like brush early in the fight. One of the Shven-Shong managed to chop off a Minotaur's arm as he kicked him to the ground with an awesome somersault kick. Before he could kill the beast with the final blow, his arm regrew, stunning the Tigren enough for the Minotaur to grab his sword and open the Tigren's belly. Another Minotaur hopped onto one of the dragons and thrust his sword through the skull and into the fleshy brain of the giant beast. The dragon's eyes closed as he slumped to the ground. Two of the combat experts cornered a Minotaur, kicking and beating it on the ground. When they grew tired, their heads were cleaved off in one, swift stroke. The last to die were the two Carcalians, speared by one ambitious Minotaur. Their sacrifice was the end of the battle and when they fell, the remaining seven climbed upon their dragons and retreated. Because the Minotaurs couldn't fly, the dragons were able to lift them to safety. Victory had come to the Minotaurs. The Tigrens had been defeated, losing five warriors and the two Carcalians. The Minotaurs marched back to the shore, and waited for their master to take them to Sphynxia.

With their tails tucked between their legs, the Shven-Shong returned to their castle. Wounded and hurt, both in pride and in body, they failed to reclaim the BellBourians that were taken as slaves. Much will have to happen to ensure victory, for immortal Minotaurs guarding the slaves will be difficult to deal with. Perhaps with unity, the Tigrens can overcome one of their greatest adversaries, and Cougran's greatest threats.

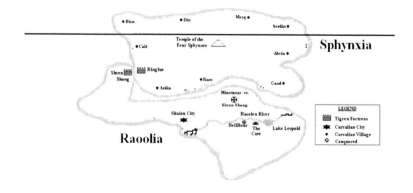

Intermission

Wars are fought over territory and resources, but the root of war always comes down to power and control: power over the people that live in the kingdom, power over the resources that are available, power over the territory that they covet. Often, a leader is elected to restore power to the people due to a corrupt inner government or economic strife. Sometimes, when this power is bestowed upon this individual, the power is misused. Sometimes, a dictator comes to power often seizing that power through force.

Such a dictator has come to power in Sphynxia. This dictator has asserted his control over six of his brothers, used his power to deny their will, and transformed their physical forms into abominations. This corruption, if not stopped, will spread like a plague over the land, infecting all that it encounters, until the people and the land wither and die.

Master RRandoll has transformed his six brothers into Minotaurs, half primate, half bull. They cannot die, their wounds heal instantly, and their limbs regrow. Fortunately, there are only six. Millions could utterly destroy the planet. However, if a weakness could be found, this enemy's advance may be thwarted...

Book 3: March of the Minotaurs

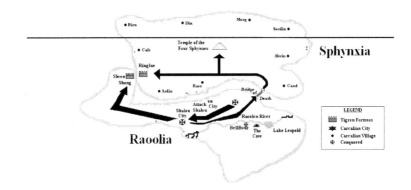

Chapter List:

Chapter 11:   Introspection...   69

Chapter 12:   Annihilation..   75

Chapter 13:   The Siege Part 1.......................................   81

Chapter 14:   The Siege Part 2.......................................   85

Chapter 15:   The Siege Part 3.......................................   89

Chapter 11: Introspection

'The personal hell of living inside a body that functions beyond your control is unbearable! My wants and wishes go unheard! My body responds to another's mind. I crave sustenance but the other denies me my existence and my commands. How can I escape from this room with no door?'

Even though Liotoch had been transformed into a ten-foot Guardian Sphynx and commanded to guard the temple at the cost of his own life, a small shimmer of his former essence still flickered in the darkness.

'The other sixty-nine Carcalians must be experiencing a similar experience. My mind craves food, yet my body does not ache from the lack of it. My essence craves sleep, yet my body isn't tired. My soul craves death, yet the "other" won't let me die. It scans the world from ten feet, a height I'm not used to. It thinks thoughts beyond my comprehension, about offensive and defensive combat, maiming to inflict suffering, and slaughter for sheer joy. Will this ever end?'

'I follow my *Master's* orders without question. I bow before *him*, for he is my *God*, yet memories of equality still linger. Memories of six other creatures, our race, called Tigren, I think, used to roam this forest. Then something changed, and now I have changed. I not only look different, I think different. My body cannot die. I cannot be permanently damaged. My only desire is to carry out my *Master's* will, killing all those that he commands me to kill, defending him and his wishes for eternity. I know no fear; I know only loyalty and my *Master's* voice, which I hear, somehow, from within. I used to be Puven, but now I am ***Minotaur*****!**'

'The carnage was absolute, the battle almost futile. How can you defeat an enemy that won't die? How do you stop a soldier that can't experience pain? We lost our two Carcalian friends with a swipe of the sword! We lost cherished friends in seconds of combat! We lost a dragon, and we lost our respect. We had to flee just to survive the slaughter! Shandowl Raulian must be told of this outrage! The Tigrens, running in the wilderness, burning down villages, is the least of our problems. Now we have an unstoppable enemy on our hands. Containment will be impossible! What are we to do? The Shandowl will know.'

The troop of shocked Tigrens flew home, battered and stunned at what they had experienced. Only half of the number that departed had returned. The trip, because they flew continuously, only took a day. They landed and entered the castle, eager to report what had occurred so a solution could be surmised.

'I have power beyond normal comprehension! The Eyes of the Four Sphinxes have unleashed the impossible to the possible! A thought can change the course of everyone's lives! I can create structures, fly, and transform life into anything I can imagine... I am unstoppable! Safety will come with control and I lack the control to ensure my security. The Academies are filled with those who will try and stop me. If they discover the source of my power, my plans will never come to fruition! I must strike while they are weak! I must create an army, but how? I cannot train and raise such an army in the time needed. But the Minotaurs could. If I can transform existing life, perhaps I can create it as well! But what shall it be? It must me invisible to the naked eye, and it must spread quickly, and infect the host rapidly in order to work. I will bestow this virus in their saliva, and by a direct bite, the virus will infect the victim, and transform it into a soldier, following the orders it is given by the Minotaurs I have created... yes... that is how it shall be!

My Minotaurs are still on Raoolia. There are over one million possible subjects in Shalou City. I must act quickly, attack first, and strike them by surprise! They won't see it coming!'

'Is this the price of treachery? Independent thought, planning, making decisions...I took them for granted. When once I was Teelor, now I am *this* cursed form, doomed to the will of another. I am a *minion*! I do not want nor wish; I do not think nor dream above my purpose: combat and carnage! Death seems like a new part of my life, chained from within, deformed from without...'

'I was second in command! Command of just a few, yes, but I had *status*! My brothers looked to me to lead while Master RRandoll was away! Master...RRandoll...just doesn't seem right. A brother, once, as well, yet now...we are subservient. I am **Minotaur**, not *Fent*. I answer to the species, not my individuality, the individuality is lost...'

'Slicing open the belly of a kinsman...I couldn't control myself! We stole a Felowitzer, sure, but killing...that...is *wrong!* We've been robbed of our identities, our wills, and our...morality. We are murderers...Babbel, the *murderer.'*

'I thought being a scout was demoralizing! I'm a mere pawn, being manipulated like a child's toy! Every moment that passes, I lose myself in this new identity, Minotaur. I have fleeting memories of who I used to be. Who was I? Sando? Yes, Sando was my name. No more. I am now an extension of my *Master*. Loyalty is without question, I cannot even think of treachery or betrayal, my mind just can't go there.'

'A slaver. A *slaver*. Using Carcalians for labor, little did I know I would become a slave myself. I am subverted to my master, just as the Carcalians were subverted to us. But now there is no *us*, there is only **He**. **He** who is all-powerful, **He** who commands, and **He** whose will shall be done. Wensha has died, I am now **Minotaur!**'

Shou 24, 5049

The Minotaurs gathered at the north shore. Master RRandoll was seen flying in the distance. He landed on a rock, and demanded that they kneel before him.

"My Minotaurs. I now bestow the reproductive power upon you and the instinct and ferocity to infect Shalou City! Bring me the bones of 10,000 dead Carcalians so I may link the two continents with a bridge, a Bridge of the Dead! The Campaign of

Carnage begins with the fall of Shalou City. Go there, bite them, they will become the Royal Army of the Temple! When all have been converted, burn the city to the ground! You six Minotaurs shall be my generals. You will command these armies on a siege on the Shven-Shong and the Ringlue Clans. Gather in formation after the city is burned. I will relay orders when this is done. Go forth, and **MULTIPLY**!"

The six Minotaur Generals marched southeast
toward Shalou City,
toward the beginning of the end of the world,
as it had been known
for over
5,000 years.

Chapter 12: Annihilation

'The screams could be heard all night long. Whatever was attacking, it was brutal, intelligent, and determined. Fear was as permeable to the city as blindness was to fog. The fear consumed us, much more so than The Leonian Crime Syndicate had our entire lives. There was no instruction by our leaders, just fear from the faceless foe. What is happening? Our only hope is escaping this terrible event by fleeing the city.'

'The horned creature is trying to smash its way into our home, our sanctuary! My pups cry out in terror... as I have over this ordeal... it's getting through! It has now smashed through the door! The creature is searching our home...oh no...he has found us! A horned, hairy creature! He has just grabbed my pup and bitten him! He tossed the screaming pup aside like a piece of garbage, and now has picked-up my second pup, bitten her, and tossed her aside! He has drawn his sword and...'

'I feel the dried blood on my neck. What has happened to me? Am I dead? No. My heart still beats; I'm still warm to the touch. There is an odd sound growing from within. My joints hurt. My head hurts, not all over, just in two spots on either side

75

of my head! I feel coarse hair sprouting from my entire body! My toes are enlarging, becoming calloused and growing together! I feel my muzzle elongating, my nostrils enlarging, my canine teeth, all but disappearing! The room, is it getting smaller? No! It's *me! I* am getting bigger! Now I am the size of those beasts that are terrorizing my people! Now I am one of those beasts! My reflection has now changed, my will is dying. My people are no longer mine, they *must* be converted! My Master's *will* be done!'

'Nothing seems to stop these wretched beasts! But why am I not dead? I took the beast's arm off and he didn't even wince! What's worse is it grew back within seconds! He came at me and bit me in the neck, yet I'm not dead! I must get back to the Leonians so they can stop these evil creatures. I feel a weird sensation coming over me!'

'The siege has lasted for two days. Endless screams, heaps of bodies. It seems that we've been overrun. I managed to slip into the forest. I must get to the Shven-Shong before there is nothing left! I hope I was able to leave without being detected.'

What the escapee did not know, was that she was being tracked. The blood and carnage had attracted the attention of a certain predator known to frequent the forest just outside the city limits. A city dweller, spending their entire lives under the protection of the city, is unaware of the dangers that lurk beyond the safety of the outer walls.

The darkness made it hard to navigate, but made it even harder for those beasts to detect her! She continued west into the forest, full of fear from the unfamiliar surroundings, not paying attention to the fact that a more serious problem was developing. After traveling for some time, she decided to rest, and then, **it** *had* **her**! Within mere minutes, the tansor's jaws were biting through the soft tissues and vertebrae in the Carcalian's neck! Its hook-like claws had prevented her escape! But the end was swift. Better to be eaten than to be damned!

Shou 29-36, 5049

As the dead began to pile-up, new converted Minotaur Warriors were assigned to collect the dead. They piled the bodies in wagons, formerly used by the residents to haul produce and other goods from place to place. Thousands not converted had been killed, per Master RRandoll's orders. The wagon trains headed east, to drop off the bodies. Some of the Minotaur Warriors would be placed on dismemberment duty, to clean the flesh off the bones, boil them, and stack them into sorted piles so that the Master could build his Bridge of Death.

After five days, the entire population of Shalou City had been slaughtered or converted. By the seventh day, all the bones had been cleaned of flesh and had been stacked in the piles as ordered.

The virus transmitted by the bites of the Minotaur Generals had not only transformed the Carcalians into Minotaur Warriors, but it had bestowed the ability onto them to create more Minotaurs, as they had been created. In each of the Minotaur's consciousness, a telepathic receiver developed so that Master RRandoll could call all his troops at will, and keep track of their movements. Master RRandoll called every Minotaur to assemble into seven groups: six groups of 132,000 troops, three to march northwest to fight the Shven-Shong, three to march across The Bridge of Death, across Sphynxia, to attack the Ringlue Clan. The remaining 200,000 would surround the Temple of the Four Sphynxes.

'Those who are on their way to attack the Shven-Shong Clan: you are to wait while the second group makes the journey to the Ringlue Clan before revealing yourselves. Each regiment of 132,000 will be commanded by a Minotaur General. I will give the order to attack when both armies are in position!'

'Go, my subjects, and remove the threat before they can mobilize against us!' said Master RRandoll through the telepathic link.

Shou 36, 5049

Fire was set to the remains of Shalou City. The Great March Began.

Shou 42, 5049

Six days passed as the march to the Shven-Shong and Ringlue Clans continued night and day. The six regiments boxed in the castles as follows: the north, west, and south edges of the Shven-Shong's Castle were surrounded as were the north, east, and south edges of the Ringlue Clan's castle. Each regiment formed into the following formations: a left wing, a main force, and right wing. Each wing contained 12,500 troops; the main force consisted of 100,000 troops. Behind the left and right wings, a left and right flank consisted of 2,500 troops. Far behind, in charge of assembling bows, arrows, ladders, bridges, clubs, hand-held battering rams, and scaffold-based battering rams were the reserve troops. The regiments remained hidden while these weapons were being completed. Master RRandoll provided the pieces of the weapons to be assembled, to alleviate the need to deforest an area before battle and to hasten the preparation time.

Shou 47, 5049

Five additional days passed as the weapons were manufactured day and night, while the soon-to-be victims were completely oblivious to the impending doom.

Chapter 13: The Siege Part 1

__Shou 48, 5049__

A glimmer of bright blue and lavender light streaked across the cool, black sky. The telepathic link between Master RRandoll and the 996,000 Minotaur Warriors made him the Chess Master of the siege, moving his soldiers into their strategic positions to guarantee the correct response from the enemy.

All twelve flanks moved into position, creating an arc behind the wings and main forces to completely surround each castle. With bows and arrows raised, the flanks began their assault, raining missiles down on the population of the castle, forcing all inhabitants to take shelter. Those who couldn't take shelter were impaled in the back, shoulder, neck, head, and legs.

At the Castle of the Shven-Shong, the western and southern forces crossed the moat and laid their ladders against the castle walls to begin their ascent to the top of the wall. Soldiers met the warriors at the tops of the ladders, their swords clashed and sparked. As the Minotaurs drove the soldiers back, more warriors came in behind to infiltrate the castle. The Tigren Soldiers were overwhelmed along the walls, driven back down the stairs or knocked off the wall altogether. The northern forces remained in formation while the southern and western forces unleashed a carnage on the Tigrens never before seen.

Castle Ringlue had a mirror-image assault: southern forces and eastern forces stormed the castle while the northern front remained on the ground. The flanks formed an arc around the wings and main forces and began their arrow assault in synchronization with the Raoolian forces.

Blood from maimed and speared Tigrens splattered and spilled down the outer walls, staining the walls and saturating the ground. Bodies rained onto the inner courtyard as more soldiers rushed to meet the onslaught of immortal assassins.

The Minotaurs infiltrated the courtyard and drove the soldiers from the southeast to the northwest corner of the castle. Those who weren't slaughtered on the way to the northern wall retreated up the steps. It was at that moment that the northern fronts crossed the moat, laid their ladders up on the wall, and up they climbed.

When the retreating troops attempted to escape up the northwest stairs, they were sandwiched between two teams of Minotaurs. Those troops were swiftly slaughtered without mercy. When all the Tigren Soldiers were nothing but rotting corpses, the Minotaur Army paused, awaiting their next order. Although every single soldier in the castle had been deployed, the entire population had not been slaughtered. The young, developing Tigrens and the older, administrative Tigrens remained inside the main castle, horrified at what they saw through the windows and heard through the walls.

The meteor that had fused power to Denzcan and created Master RRandoll also saturated his mind with the knowledge of destruction, pain, fear, and military assault tactics. It also detached and dismantled his emotions along with his morality. For once the meteorite's absolute power saturated his cells, the concept of good disappeared.

"Who are they Master Hann?" asked the cub.

"I'm not sure, but they fight and destroy as one. They all seem to know what the others are doing and they react accordingly. They have fighting skills and abilities that I've never seen before. Look, that one's arm was just severed, yet he's grown a new one and surprised his adversary. That ability is unnatural. Come, we must hurry. I'm sure the castle is surrounded."

"Yes, Master."

The two descended several floors to a corridor. At the end of the corridor, Master Hann pressed a combination of stones, which revealed a hidden door. The two hurried inside, just as the door slid shut behind them.

"Where are we going Master?" asked the cub.

"This passageway leads under the moat, into a hidden part of the forest. We can escape the total destruction of our Clan without being detected by that army. My instincts tell me that the army won't be looking for escapees. They'll think they've won, and that is our advantage."

At the end of the corridor there was a ladder leaning against the wall, leading to a door in the ceiling. They climbed the ladder, pulled the handle backward, and the hatch door swung downward.

"Quickly. We must find a pekall to get far from here. Keep a sharp eye."

"But Master, wouldn't a dragon be much more suitable for travel? I mean, pekalls are rather small for us, well, you."

"Ah, but you forget. Just because I'm mature, doesn't mean I can't revert to my Carcalian form. Remember, I was trained as you will be to control the metamorphosis. We will be less threatening disguised as Carcalians."

"I see two of them right up that tree, Master!"

"Well, come on, up the tree, then."

Chapter 14: The Siege Part 2

__Shou 48, 5049__

Thousands of Minotaur Warriors with battering rams began their relentless pounding on the barricades at Castle Shven-Shong. Those who weren't pounding at the doors began pounding on the walls with massive logs that swung from scaffolds. These scaffolds were built during the siege and brought in through the front drawbridge to get through the stone walls of the main complex of the Shven-Shong.

The Ringlue Castle, however, was not as well barricaded, and within minutes, the Minotaurs flooded the complex. Warriors ran through the hallways in search of their next victims. Up staircases, down elevators they searched, but the buildings were abandoned. Had they all been slaughtered? Where were the elders? Where were the yearlings?

"We must hurry. These armies are the seed of pure evil. All of our warriors have been cut-down like harvest grain. We will split-up into four groups and meet at the Sacred Hallow. Go." said General Janell.

'That's odd. There should be two-thirds of the population left to slaughter. There must be underground exits,' thought the lead Minotaur.

The command was sent to the reserves to search the surrounding forests. Search parties fanned out in all directions to track down the elusive refugees.

The old and young screamed in terror, paralyzed by the slashing swords of the Minotaurs. The barricades had fallen, and their swords had severed heads and speared lungs of young and old alike. Chunks of flesh flew from the shoulders of old Tigrens who had lived over eighty years! They had trained generations of Tigren youths how to control their rage and how to channel that rage into combat for the good of themselves and the entertainment of all Cougrans.

Yearlings were hacked to pieces, old males and females fell to the ground, spilling blood in gallons all over the cold stone floor. All were killed regardless of status, training, age, all except for the Shandowl. The Shandowl was captured alive and placed in chains. The only known survivor of the Shven-Shong Clan, Shandowl Raulian, was tied backwards to a tree and whipped into unconsciousness.

In Sphynxia, the search parties were vigorously combing the forests, looking under every bush, in every tree, under every rock, yet the survivors eluded them. The only way to ensure that they weren't hiding right under their noses was to set fire to the forests. This would ensure that the survivors would be driven to the shores, where thousands of troops would be waiting for them.

Shou 49, 5049

"I think it's safe to come out. The troops have passed."

The northern group emerged from the hidden exit and began their trek to the Sacred Hallow. A Minotaur search party soon picked up their trail and relayed the telepathic message to Master RRandoll. They were told to track them, but not to engage. If there were more survivors, they would most likely be moving toward a central meeting place.

The south, east, and west teams emerged from their hidden exits scattered in the dense forest. Smoke had begun to blow in from the south. Could it be fire? But how? There had been no storms to generate thunderbolts. If not from the sky, then it must be from those beasts!

In total, 400 Tigrens escaped from the assault on Castle Ringlue. What the Tigrens didn't know, was that more Minotaurs were on the way, now numbering 1500!

All four parties met at the Sacred Hallow.

"We may have to keep moving," said Vectan, of the Southern Group, to Manz, of the Northern Group.

"Why do you say such a thing? Those beasts are at the castle!" replied Manz.

"We smelled fire to the southwest. No storms. No thunder bolts. It must be an effort to flush us out."

A rustle in the bushes stopped all conversation and thought.

The search party finally caught up with the northern group. They waited in the bushes until the remaining 1200 troops had arrived. But a mistake by a restless Minotaur tipped their quarry off...

Chapter 15: The Siege Part 3

Shou 49, 5049

"Flee! Scatter into the woods! If they catch you, they will kill you, or worse! Survive at all costs!"

One thousand, five-hundred Minotaur Warriors rushed the crowd of Tigrens to quench this threat to their takeover. Tigrens scattered in all directions, many, due to old age or youth were cut-down in the initial rush. The pursuit carried on into the forest, the Minotaurs drove the survivors north toward the shore! An additional 1500 troops were waiting for the fleeing refugees.

"Master Hann, do you think they know we've escaped?" asked the boy.

"One never knows, young Bengal. The intelligence and control of that army is unprecedented. They function as one. They cannot be destroyed by normal means. When we get to Nidia and contact the Clushpow Clan, we will put our heads together to try to solve this disturbing chain of events. They are best prepared to handle this new threat to us all. They are the best sword masters in the world, and have the largest population. They are our best hope for defeating this evil."

The two caught their pekalls, and Master Hann reverted to his Carcalian form. (Bengal is a pre-pubescent Tigren and has not yet reached The Age of Shen Long). They removed some vines and made a makeshift bit from a branch cleared of its bark. They harnessed the pekalls and took off toward the Nidian Capital.

The fastest of the refugees and some of the smallest were able to cut through the bushes and undergrowth faster than the bulky, 10 foot Minotaurs. The initial dash of 400 refugees yielded 350 survivors, but because the Minotaurs don't tire, the survivors' numbers dwindled quickly. Only fifty made it to the shore, and all were cut down when they arrived, with the exception of the Shandowl, who, like Shandowl Raulian, was captured alive. He, too, was whipped into unconsciousness after being tied to a tree.

'Bring the Shandowls to the Temple. They will have a personal purpose in my presence. Form a barrier on all four sides of each castle, 20 rows thick. An additional 1,000 will occupy the interior of the castles. The remaining 779,640 troops will return to the Temple.'

The requisitioned 217,360 Minotaur Warriors took their places in the castle. When the last Warrior was in position, they all turned to stone! The active troops, each group of 389,820, took the captured Shandowl, tied him to a pole, and carried him on the shoulders of two warriors. Master RRandoll had given specific instructions to deliver the Shandowls to The Temple of the Four Sphynxes.

The initial battle is over. Both castles are occupied, their former occupants slaughtered, their Shandowls captured, which means that the power centers of two continents are subdued. Five more remain. The larger continents contain more castles, more villages, and more seeds for future troops. But they also create the possibility of defeat.

The Shandowls of the Shven-Shong and Ringlue Clans arrived at the Temple, the ultimate symbol of their destruction lay before him in these leaders. A voice whispered in his mind, something new to Master RRandoll. Images of this statement followed, and he had the complete picture of what would become of the Shandowls! The two were removed from their poles and made to stand. With a wave of the hand, both turned to stone! He opened the ground and set their mineralized bodies in the hole, and covered them with soil, hiding them from sight. The disturbed vegetation was returned to its previous condition, as if nothing had happened. Now, with the total annihilation of the Shven-Shong and Ringlue Clans, work could begin on destroying the others!

But as powerful as Master RRandoll was, he wasn't powerful enough to sense the escape of Master Hann and Bengal, who were the last of the Shven-Shong Clan. With the complete slaughter of the Tigrens and Carcalians on Raoolia, Master RRandoll would be free to rule Raoolia and Sphynxia without interference. It seemed, to Master RRandoll, that Cougran itself was an attainable goal, which he could rule as he saw fit! There he could work on leaving this world to conquer the next!

But that may take centuries...

Book 4: The Ripple Effect

Chapter List:

Chapter 16:   Deconstruction..   94

Chapter 17:   Ambush!..   98

Chapter 18:   Deforestation & Rebirth.......................................   102

Chapter 19:   The Fruit of Evil..   108

Chapter 20:   The Summit of Nidia..   112

Chapter 16: Reconstruction

Shou 48, 5049

As the Minotaurs tore down Castle Ringlue brick by brick, the fires that had been set to trap the fleeing Ringlue Clan continued to burn. As the wildfires spread, animals were driven out of the forest, away from the ensuing danger. Animals that were normally solitary found themselves partnered with unfamiliar species running from the non-discriminating flames. Predator and prey were fleeing together.

Shou 49, 5049

The dismantlement continued. Block after block was dropped into the Straits of Raoolia, off the western shore of Sphynxia. Minotaurs did not question the orders of their Master, regardless of how insane the plans may have been. Dismantling castles block by block, taking care only to crack the mortar to release the blocks was quite logically mad, when Master RRandoll had the power to build temples with just his mind. The madman was creating another bridge, using his enemy's castles to do it, or so it seemed.

Shou 51, 5049

The flight across the Sea of FeRalia was met with intense winds, rolling seas, and thunderous storms. The journey across the sea began just before first light, giving the pekalls the maximum amount of daylight Cougran can offer. They had only 6 ½ hours of sunlight, which was barely enough time. Pekalls are gliders, not hard fliers, so the updrafts had to be navigated, which meant an indirect route over the ocean.

When darkness began to envelop the sky, the pekalls descended. The hollow bones of the pekalls that made them such good gliders also aided in flotation. Master Hann and Bengal realized that they'd have to wait out the night floating on their pekalls, when they didn't see land over the horizon.

The night was long, cold, and windy. The relentless up and down of the waves made both travelers rather ill. When dawn broke through the darkness, the refugees were up and away.

Shou 61, 5049

In an instant, one-hundred the Minotaur Warriors stationed around Castle Shven-Shong snapped to life from their mineralized slumber. A search began for every ounce of metal they could muster from the occupied castles. They located several hundred pounds of metal and went to the forges in the castles to begin their work.

The hammering and pounding began as soon as the metal was hot enough to shape. Pieces were hammered together to form spikes, chisels, and heads for sledgehammers. Smaller, handheld hammer heads were made to accompany the chisels. When thousands of these metal pieces were completed, they were fastened onto wooden handles, made into sledgehammers, handheld hammers, and chisels.

The remaining stone Minotaur Warriors snapped to life and lined-up to arm themselves, not with swords and battering rams, but with the newly made chisels and hammers.

Shou 66, 5049

The Minotaurs went to work, carefully breaking up the mortar holding the stones of the castle together. Those not chiseling and hammering began picking the stones up and handing it to the next Minotaur, forming a chain all the way down to the ground, extending east to the Straits of Raoolia. The outer wall was the first to go. Each of the blocks were piled one upon another, until they broke the surface of the water. The same occurred at Castle Ringlue; each block was removed and dropped into the sea. It took 3 days of non-stop, round the clock work, but when the walls were completely removed, demolition ceased.

Shou 69, 5049

Master RRandoll appeared at the Shven-Shong's former castle. He visualized the location of where their document and record chamber was in his mind and appeared there. With his mental powers, he removed every scrap of paper and every record from the chamber. They began reappearing on the second floor of the Temple of the Four Sphynxes until the record room had been completely emptied. He reappeared on the outside of the Ringlue Clan's Castle. He located their record room and removed all records that they had kept, and deposited them one by one next to the Shven-Shong's documents on the second floor of the Temple. When all those records had been removed, the Minotaurs resumed their work on dismantling the castles and dropping the blocks into the sea.

The sighting of land meant that Master Hann and Bengal had reached the province of Shenlow-Maux in southern Felinia. The famished travelers landed to eat and rest in the forest. The journey will be long. Nidia is on the other side of the planet, and they were taking the overland route, which would be safer, but will take much longer to complete. The Shenlowpow Clan, which occupies Felinia, is a large clan, but less likely to care about others' affairs and much less likely to welcome outsiders. The 30,000-mile trip to Nidia would be necessary…and arduous.

Chapter 17: Ambush!

Shou 69, 5049

Master RRandoll, until now, had not been aware that Sphynxia had been populated with Carcalians. In fact, there were nine villages in existence on Sphynxia, no bigger than BellBour. Master RRandoll saw an opportunity to expand his military might beyond the one million he had already under his command. This attack must be swift, simultaneous and soon, before news spread to the villages that their Tigren protectors were no more.

'Attention my armies. Nine-hundred of you will bring this continent to its knees. Invade and surround the coastal villages and increase your ranks with your bite! Along the northern coast, the villages of Birn, Din, Merg, and Sordin have to be taken. On the east cost there is Abvin. Along the southern coast there is Cand, Rase, and Ardin. On the west coast there is Calt. Recruit the population with your infectious gift and then burn the villages down to the ground. Go forth, my minions, bring glory to the RRandollian Empire!'

The Minotaur Warriors split into nine groups of one-hundred each. They marched at equivalent rates in order to arrive at the villages simultaneously. The warriors hid in the bushes until nightfall, when they'd have the greatest advantage.

Night fell on the Sphynxians. Unbeknownst to them, they would no longer enjoy the harmony they once did. Petty squabbles over property or monetary concerns would be a thing of the past. When darkness had enveloped the land in the cloak of night, the Minotaurs swept in from all sides!

Doors were kicked in. Nurseries were raided. Mothers, fathers, yearlings, elders were all bitten, none were spared. The changes occurred within minutes of each bite. One-hundred turned into one-thousand, then two-thousand, and on and on until every last Carcalian in every last village had been infected and transformed into Minotaur Warriors.

Shou 76, 5049

All the villages had been built using the most readily available materials. Unfortunately, for the former inhabitants, they were easily burned. Torches passed from warrior to warrior and from home to home. Nothing escaped the fires. Destruction was total. An additional 11,500 warriors were added to the already formidable army of immortal Minotaurs.

The villages formed a ring of fire around the continent, igniting everything surrounding the villages. The new fires met with the existing fires burning on the western side of the continent. Now ¾ of the continent was ablaze. Master RRandoll conjured a continental rainstorm that quieted the fires to nothing but a mere fog. Blackened ash stretched hundreds of miles on the west side of the continent and in a ring around its shoreline.

The Minotaurs that had just been created marched inland toward the Temple of the Four Sphynxes. Their wills had joined the collective consciousness of Master RRandoll, now including 1.2 million Minotaurs and 70 Sphinxes.

Shou 71, 5049

The ground began shaking. A terrible thunder bellowed from within the planet. The seafloor beneath the Straits of Raoolia began breaking through the surface of the narrow body of water separating Sphynxia from Raoolia! The mighty wall of water rippled south, then east, toward the Sybeerian Ocean. The millions of gallons of water rushed eastward, combining with the Sybeerian Ocean, heading straight for western Nidia and Cougranada!

Sixty-foot swells rolled toward the Nidian coast at 500 miles per hour. Cougranada received minor ten-foot swells. The Nidian shore was pounded relentlessly with the after effects of this huge shift in land mass. When the 60-foot swells reached the continental shelf, the water climbed to a staggering 200 feet!

The land rose so fast that the planet could barely cope with the shock! The upheaval snapped the Bridge of Death into splinters of bone. The earthquakes knocked the Minotaurs to the ground that had been so diligent at dismantling the castles. Raoolia and Sphynxia had now become one landmass! Millions of gallons of water had been displaced. The Nidian coast was devastated. Some 6,000 miles of coastline was submerged under 26 hours of horrific, 200-foot waves. Water washed into the forest, wiping out hundreds of thousands of trees, washing debris all the way to the Cougrinium-rich Mountains! Sphynxia had merged with Raoolia, giving birth to the super-continent of New Raoolia!

Chapter 18: Deforestation & Rebirth

Shou 71, 5049

Master Hann and Bengal's journey across the Felinian continent was long and tiresome. They decided to find a village along the shore to rest for a few days. They had been flying nonstop for 20 days straight and their pekalls were becoming temperamental. They sighted a village and glided to its entrance.

"Who's there?" the guard announced to the landing of the travelers.

"We are travelers in need of rest and supplies. We ask for rest and refuge while our pekalls recover from our journey."

"Where do you hail from?" asked the guard.

"We're travelers from Raoolia. We are on our way to Nidia to see the sites and visit the cities that abound the continent," replied Master Hann.

"We grant you privilege to our hospitality and rest, great travelers. Please enjoy food, drink, rest, and some supplies to help you complete your journey. Please, enter and enjoy."

"What is your village called?" asked Bengal.

"Ah, my young friend, you have arrived at Cheegran," answered the guard.

Master Hann and Bengal walked through the arched entrance and were led to a place where they could store their pekalls for some much-needed rest. The travelers were shown to their rooms, and were granted a chaperone to tour the village and seek out supply huts and eateries.

Shou 76, 5049

'This continent is now in my sole possession. The life that lives here will now serve my purpose: to guard the land from the perversion of the Tigren Clans.'

A black ooze flowed from the pyramid, through the soil and into every living, breathing organism in contact with the ground. Trees began losing their leaves, dropping branches, and finally, cracking in half and falling to the ground. Pekalls began morphing into flying, fire-breathing drakells. Tonias grew horrid, jagged teeth. Instead of being their usual, omnivorous, fruit and insect eating selves, their behavior turned predatory and violent toward each other. Family groups, common to the species, disbanded out of mistrust and violence. Tansors grew from being 12-foot beasts, to 40-foot, snarling, howling monstrosities!

From the dead trees emerged bipedal, carnivorous reptiles with three-inch pointed teeth and six-inch claws. These creatures became Master RRandoll's personal predasaurs. The dead leaves spawned hordes of bloodthirsty flying insects with six-inch wingspans.

As the black ooze made its way through the soil, transferring its menacing influence to everything in its grasp, the western side of the newly formed super-continent, along with the former locations of the Sphynxian Villages became known as the Land of the Dead. The ooze killed every living thing in this area, damned each living essence between the physical and spiritual realms in a ghostly form known as the wraith. In the physical world, wraiths appear as skeletons, wrapped in a black, hooded cloak to hide their true forms. They move about in a ghostly blue fog, patrolling the Land of the Dead, looking for life to feed upon. Each wraith was damned to exist in a jealous rage, jealous of the life that they had lost, enraged because they can't move on to the next life. Either the life that the wraiths steal can be fed upon, or the life force could be added to their ranks, trapping more souls in their maddening existence. Regardless, any life that entered their domain would be physically ripped to pieces and the life force would be removed from the physical world!

Realizing the unlimited and infinite ends of his newfound power, Master RRandoll decided that dismantling the Shven-Shong and Ringlue Clans' castles seemed unnecessary. The Pall of Death had completed its infectious journey across the newly formed super-continent. The Minotaurs charged with the task were assigned patrol duty. Since the wraiths could cover half of the super-continent, the Minotaurs were teleported to the southeastern edge of the continent to protect it from possible invaders approaching from Cougranada. The interior was covered by the mutated tansors, and the southeastern shore was covered by the predasaurs. The mutated Tonias along with the drakells were in charge of patrolling the skies for any aerial attack.

The scores of predatory animals were programmed to attack any Carcalian or Tigren setting foot on the land. If they landed on the western, northwestern, or northern shore, the wraiths would swarm about them, disrupt their sense of time, make them go mad, and then reduce them to a pile of stinking, rotting meat!

The massive tidal waves that devastated Nidia's western shore alerted the attention of the Clushpow Clan. All of the top members of each of the fifteen castles were summoned to discuss the alarming events that occurred to trigger such a disaster. No known natural occurrence had ever been recorded in the 5,000 years of recorded history that could account for the complete and utter devastation felt in this region. Surely, with all of their combined knowledge, and interactive cooperation, a solution to this outrage could be discovered.

The solace of being amongst a community again was a welcomed distraction from the traumatic events that had recently transpired. Bengal enjoyed being around the Carcalians. He knew that Tigrens originate from Carcalian mothers and fathers, but he had never dreamed he'd be able to interact with them! Master Hann also seemed to enjoy the distraction. He was more often the serious type, but given the change of environment, and the need for refuge, Master Hann decided to relax and take advantage of the Carcalian hospitality.

Shou 81, 5049

The Minotaur Warriors would be at the ready, patrolling the perimeter of the Temple of the Four Sphynxes, backing up the Sphinx Army in hundreds of squads. They would also cover the southern shore, taking up the area not covered by predasaurs or tansors. The 40-foot tansors patrolled the southern interior section of the continent in packs of 10. Each patrol had an alpha male and alpha female. Before they were infected, they were solitary predators. The mutated Tonias covered the skies, looking for approaching Tigrens on dragon-back. The drakells hid in the forest as a backup to the Tonias, in the event they were overwhelmed. If anyone were foolish enough to approach the eastern shore, the reptilian bipeds and bloodthirsty insects would squelch that threat.

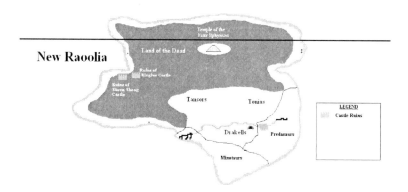

New Raoolia

Temple of the
Four Sphynxes

Land of the Dead

Ruins of
Kinghu Castle

Ruins of
Shrou Shrug
Castle

Tansors   Tonias

Drakells   Predasaurs

Minotaurs

LEGEND

Castle Ruins

Chapter 19: The Fruit of Evil

Shou 21-76, 5049

As power began to course through Denzcan's veins during his gradual transformation from Denzcan to Master RRandoll, subtle changes to his body occurred. They were slow at first, and as he used more and more power from the meteorite, unbeknownst to Master RRandoll, his body began to deteriorate.

His eyes started to sink further and further into his skull. The flesh in his face gradually began to diminish, and his eyes grew red with the evil that flowed through him. By the time of the great tidal wave, skin and hair began flaking away from his bones. As he took more and more power into his being, it took more and more life from his body.

The moral center of his mind was the conduit from which this evil flowed. It quickly dissolved his brain matter, and took control of his primitive brain. The power corrupted his sense of right and wrong, commanded his breathing and heart regulator, and gradually rotted the flesh and hair from his bones.

What started out as a red pigment to the iris eventually became a glowing light in place of his eyes. The skin on his fingers shrunk until only bony claws remained. All of his vegetarian teeth loosened and fell out of his mouth, littering the ground along with his hair and dried flesh. All that remained were his two-inch canine teeth, which added to his gruesome appearance.

The changes progressed unnoticed to Master RRandoll. He was so focused on his manifestations and transformations to the living creatures and the land that he was unable to see the damage being done to his own body.

After the merging of Sphynxia and Raoolia, he came out of his trance long enough to realize the change in his appearance. The horror was absolute! He suddenly became aware of the cost of using this power: he was now deformed and in incredible pain! The skeletal being conjured a mirror so he could see the source of his pain, and when he saw himself, he collapsed in a heap of sobs and cries.

Some time passed, then he picked himself up from his depressive heap and his own madness drove him to laughter. He inhaled the full power of the Eyes of the Four Sphynxes and turned it on himself. The futility of this use of the power was realized quickly. He could not heal with this power. All this power could do was destroy. He now knew the true cost for such a power.

The pain from his transformation was constant and severe. His gums burned and throbbed at the loss of his teeth. The glow that emanated from his eye sockets had burned and rotted his eyeballs down to the optic nerve. This burning pain from the lack of eyes and the lack of lids was enhanced by any light that he was exposed to. His lack of fat, skin, and hair made the remaining muscles and tendons shiver from the eternal cold that he felt.

He sat down on his throne, located on the bottom level of his seven level step pyramid temple. RRandoll's suffering would never end, as long as he continued to use this power. Was the power controlling Denzcan's will, or was Master RRandoll just an outgrowth of Denzcan's dark side? How connected had he become to this power? Would he survive outside its influence? Time to test it out.

Shou 77, 5049

Master RRandoll floated through the layers of his temple, and out through the sunroof. He flew to the west, toward the wraiths, and when he crossed into the Land of the Dead, the pain of his affliction subsided. His flesh slowly returned to his body. His teeth reappeared as the throbbing ceased. The burning in his eyes ceased as the glow was replaced with the return of his eyeballs. He then descended to the ground. It seemed that in this land, his Tigren form would return and his pain would cease.

All of a sudden, a sharp pain struck his chest like a bolt of lightening! The shocking pain drove him to his knees. His heart began to slow, and fire shot through his veins. The agony of this sensation was greater than any pain that he had suffered at the hands of this alien power!

He summoned his wraiths to his aid, and two of them rose out of the cold, blue fog. They had foreseen this moment, for the spiritual plane exists outside of the constraints of time. They had made a special hooded robe that would preserve their Master's decaying body so he could remain in proximity to his power and not rot to dust. This hooded robe, created from materials from the spiritual plane, helped Master RRandoll defy the decay brought on by this excessive power.

The wraiths dressed their Creator in this robe and carried him to the edge of their land. Master RRandoll's pain ceased and the power surged through his body as soon has he crawled beyond the wraiths' borders. He returned to his Temple, descending to the lowest level, and sat upon his throne. He now had the ultimate power, without the price of pain! Even though he had to stay in the Temple, probably for all eternity, he considered the trade acceptable. He would reign over this land, and soon, the world!

And what a fruitful reign it would be!

Chapter 20: The Summit of Nidia

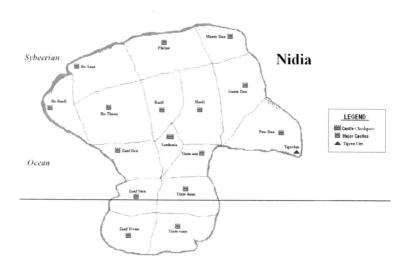

Shou 79, 5049

The great journey to the head of the Clushpow Clan's power center was underway. Delegates from each of the 15 Academies were sent to the continental capital Sandonia. As soon as news spread of the great catastrophe, it was up to the Tigrens to take whatever measures necessary to discover the origins of this disaster.

Several decades ago, the capital of Nidia was established in the center of the continent so each sub-clan would be equidistant to the capital. During the annual games, being equidistant to the capital made arriving on time quite convenient.

The Inter-Continental Games are held during the first 12 weeks of the mating month, Estrella, at the capitals of Felinia, Nidia, and Cougranada.

The convenience of centrality amongst the sub-clans was ever apparent in this time of crisis. Each castle was no more than a 3-day flight from the capital.

The arrival of the delegates was met with swift attention. Once all the delegates arrived and were settled in their respective suites, the meetings began.

"The Nidian High Council recognizes the delegate from the Western Clans. Please relay what you've observed of our situation," announced Verdand.

"I, Septura, of the Clush-Bow will report the events that have transpired."

"Please continue," said Verdand.

"Thank you, Highness. Our scouts have surveyed the entire Sybeerian coast; the extent of the damage is unparalleled. Witnesses tell of the disappearance of the sea for several minutes. The fish and sea-life not used to the open air flopped around on rocky soil and bare ground. The wall of water grew from the emptiness, and rose as tall as a mountain for as far as the eye could see. The water uprooted trees, washed away the sand, and flooded lands that have never seen the ocean. The younger trees

113

that were uprooted crashed into the ancient ones, breaking trunks that have stood for hundreds of years, as if they were mere twigs.

Each successive wave of water reached further inland. As the water would recede, giant boulders appeared in their retreat. Wave after wave crashed against the shore from dusk to dawn and from dawn to dusk. Water still stands where there were once extensive beaches. We are grateful that no Carcalians live near the shore. No one would have survived."

"Thank you for your observations. This troubles me greatly," said Verdand in a grave voice. "The Council recognizes the delegates of the Southern clans."

"I, Dond, of the Clush-Zanf-den Clan thank you for this opportunity to speak."

"Please proceed," replied Verdand.

"Thank you, Highness. The Zanfs confirm the report given by the Clush-Bow delegate. Our scouts witnessed massive swells moving between Nidia and Cougranada. Our western shores were devastated as the Clush-Bow Clans' were. Unlike the west, however, we had Carcalian villages on our shores. A total of six villages were completely washed away! A seventh village was destroyed, but they evacuated in time. Thousands of Carcalians are dead! We must discover the source of this madness!" reported Dond in a heated tone.

"It seems the mountains protected the interior of the continent from this destructive force. We did not see any damage, but our sympathies extend to the hardships faced by the Zanf's people. Is anyone opposed to an aerial survey of the globe? Certainly there must be damage elsewhere on the planet," said Verdand.

"The Chair recognizes the delegate of the Clush-Pow-Don," said Pensha.

"Thank you, Highness," said Cronk. "We request permission to send a large-scale air squadron to survey the globe. We ask for thirty-five pilots from each sector to accompany and corroborate our findings. We wish to launch from the port city Tigerian and fan out in eight directions. This will enable us to cover Lexinia's coast, Taradynia, Felinia, Sphynxia, Raoolia, and Cougranada. The more help we receive the more thorough our search can be," he suggested.

"Is everyone in agreement?" asked Verdand.

"Yes," they stated in unison.

"Then the aerial survey is approved. You may proceed with this survey and report your findings to this Council in exactly 1 month. Thirteen weeks should give you enough time to circumnavigate the planet, shouldn't it Master Cronk?" asked Pensha.

"Yes, Highness, it should," replied Cronk.

"Then all is in agreement. Meeting adjourned," announced Verdand.

Shou 82, 5049

The clans returned to their respective castles and had their reports with their individual councils. The damage was documented and the pilots reported to Tigerian's launch point on the eastern peninsula.

Shou 84, 5049

The search for the origin of this natural disaster began with the dawn of the new day.

Book 5: Expedition

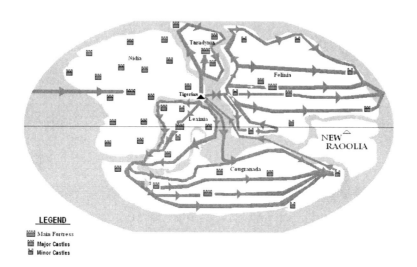

Chapter List:

Chapter 21:   Aerial Expedition.. 118

Chapter 22:   Meeting of the Minds... 124

Chapter 23:   Mystery of the Red Rain.................................. 128

Chapter 24:   Raoolian Raid.. 132

Chapter 25:   Another Piece of the Puzzle............................. 136

Chapter 21: Aerial Expedition

Shou 84-86, 5049

Five flights of dragons and their pilots converged on the Tigren City of Tigerian, located on the eastern peninsula of Nidia. This would be the launch point for the greatest aerial expedition in the planet's entire history! Five-hundred twenty-five dragon fliers assembled to discover the full global impact of the massive 200-foot tidal waves that devastated western Nidia. They were all briefed on the mission, its scope, and the timeline in which the survey had to be completed.

The horns sounded, marking the commencement of the expedition! Dragons took to the air and fanned out in all directions! They divided into four main squadrons, splitting into small flights to cover as much territory as possible. Three flights of thirty flew northeast toward the Taradynian coast. Two flights fanned out to circle the continent and one flew over the interior. While the two flights navigated the perimeter, the central flight landed at the Svintz Clan's Castle. They inquired about any unusual activity, but the clan had not experienced any unnatural events. The delegation reported the events that had transpired and the damage to the Nidian coast. The party departed with no more information than they had arrived with. They met the two flights surveying the east and west coasts on the northern shore.

No damage was found along the coast or on the interior of the continent.

Three flights of 30 flew south toward Lexinia to survey its coasts and interior. Unlike the expedition to Taradynia, the 10-foot swells that were sighted by the Southern Clan grew to 50-foot swells when it passed between the continents. Tidal waves swept into the Lexinians and wiped out twelve villages on the coast. Because Lexinia is mostly temperate and tropical forest, the water flowed inland several hundred miles. A third of the continent, on the southern side, was flooded. Just as the powerful tidal forces uprooted trees on Nidia, so too was the case with Lexinia.

The flight of dragons covering the central overland survey met with the Maestry Clan at their castle, located on the equator, in the center of the continent. The Maestry Clan explained the damage that occurred to the southern third of their lands. While no loss of life was reported, populations from 12 Carcalian villages fled to the interior to escape the rising water. The three flights rejoined to share the physical data with the verbal information collected from the Maestry Clan.

The three flights that surveyed Lexinia met with five flights of dragon fliers to survey Cougranada. The continent of Cougranada stretches from the southern coast of Nidia all the way to the southwestern coast of Raoolia, which is on the other side of the 40,000-mile planet.

The 80 dragon fliers that met on the southern edge of Nidia noticed that several miles of coastline was underwater. Trees stuck out of the flooded landscape like marker buoys indicating the edge of the forest. Three flights took the northern coast, three took the southern coast, and two covered the interior.

Cougranada received minimal damage. The only part of Cougranada that had seen tidal forces was the western tip. The 20 dragon fliers surveying the interior stopped at the Shou Clan's Castle. They confirmed reports of damage to the west coast, but added that rumbling could be heard coming from the northeast. They speculated that there could have been some geologic activity in Raoolia or even as far north as Sphynxia. The Shou Clan was thanked for their time and the 20 fliers mounted-up and headed for the rendezvous point on the eastern shore. A flight would be sent back to Nidia to report their findings and speculation. The other 70 would wait for instructions upon the flight's return.

Shou 84-87, 5049

While the surveys of Lexinia and Cougranada were taking place, the remaining 400 dragon fliers were assigned to Felinia. Felinia is a massive continent, and it would require 40 flights to circumnavigate the immense body of land. They would meet at the eastern tip, review their findings, and get back to Nidia in time for the summit.

The 40 flights split into four groups: ten flights would cover the north, ten would cover the northern middle section, ten covered the middle southern section, and ten covered the southern shore. One flight from the northern middle and one flight from the southern middle would meet with the Shenlowpow Clan. Their castle is located well into the interior of the continent.

No damage was reported by the Shenlowpow Clan. All of their villages remained as prosperous as they always had been. The suggestion by the Clushpow that any event could have occurred seemed preposterous. The thought of some massive tidal wave coming from the Sybeerian Ocean seemed ludicrous at best. The delegates were dismissed out of hand and asked to leave, never bother them with this type of gibberish again. The cold reception was expected, but the delegates respected their hosts' wishes and left respectfully. They continued onto the rendezvous point on the eastern shore.

Shou 101-106, 5049

The expedition of the southern flights, however, came upon two pekalls flying east, toward Nidia. Two Carcalians were riding the pekalls, which would have gone unnoticed if one of them had not flagged the Tigren surveyors down. They met in a grassy field just north of the equator.

"State your business Carcalians, quickly, we are on an important mission," said Fando.

"We are not Carcalians," said Master Hann, as he metamorphosized into his true form. "We are the last of the Shven-Shong Clan. All of our people were wiped out by an army of warriors that appeared from all directions. We were able to escape, but just barely. We are on our way to your capital to relay the disturbing events, so that we may destroy this evil that now plagues our land."

"We are part of a massive expedition sent by the Nidian High Council. Five flights of dragon fliers made up of a collaboration of all the Nidian Provinces are doing a survey of this planet. We are trying to discover what kind of geologic event could have caused such catastrophic damage on our shores and to the other continents as well," replied Fando.

"May we accompany you on your journey to rendezvous with your other fliers? Our pekalls are ill suited for such a long distance journey. We would be most helpful in your quest, and we have much information about this enemy," petitioned Master Hann.

"Very well. We must meet with the others." Fando turned to the pilots, "Mount-up troops. To the east coast we must go!" Turning back to Master Hann, he said, "Leave your pekalls and climb aboard. We've lost precious time," he added.

The flock of dragon fliers rendezvoused with the remaining teams on the east coast of Felinia. All were informed of the extermination of the Shven-Shong and how the attacking force regrew limbs. The expedition flew east across the Sybeerian Ocean and landed at the Clushpow's Fortress in Sandonia. Master Hann and Bengal went inside the castle. The guards ushered them toward the High Council Chamber. Afterwards, they were escorted to an apartment to wait for the other dragon teams to relay their findings.

One of the flights that had returned from Cougranada was sent to retrieve the remaining flights stationed just south of Raoolia. They all regrouped at Tigerian to report the extensive damage they had witnessed during the 12-week survey. Master Cronk then took the information to the Clushpow Fortress to inform the High Council of his findings.

The truth about the events in Raoolia and Sphynxia will be told, and the ones responsible will atone for their misdeeds...

Chapter 22: Meeting of the Minds

Shou 109, 5049

"Come to order, all, come to order," announced Verdand. "The summit of the Delegation of the Clushpow Clan will come to order. We of the Nidian High Council will hear your report of the state of our planet. We will also hear from our honored guests of the Shven-Shong Clan, hailing from Raoolia."

"The Council recognizes the delegate of the Clush-Pow-Don Clan, and organizer of the Great Expedition, Master Cronk. Please state your report," announced Pensha.

"Thank you, Highness. The results of the survey has shown extensive damage localized to the west coast of Nidia, the northwestern peninsula of Cougranada, and the southern third of Lexinia. We suspect the origin of this damage was from Raoolia, although our effort to send a flight to that area was thwarted by our guests. It is likely that some geologic activity has occurred in Raoolia," reported Master Cronk.

"Why was the suspected disturbance on Raoolia left to speculation?" asked Verdand.

"Well," explained Master Cronk, "when we stumbled upon the last two survivors of the Shven-Shong Clan, we decided to return and discuss what they have encountered."

Gasps filled the room. A look of horror crossed all the participants. Shock, confusion, awe, and demand for more information bellowed from the audience.

"Come to order! Come to order! Please, all will be answered in good time. Please, continue your report Master Cronk," said Verdand.

"At this time, Highness, I wish to turn the floor over to our guest, Master Hann of the Shven-Shong," he stated.

"We appreciate your audience," said Master Hann. "We come to you after a series of terrible events. An army has attacked our castle and has decimated our people. Young Bengal and I are the only known survivors. What is most disturbing is that there was no apparent leader to the assault, yet they all functioned as one. During the battle, several of the mysterious creatures were maimed and their limbs regrew in seconds, to the detriment of the warrior who took the limb. They attacked in the cloak of darkness, scaled our walls, surrounded our exits to exploit our fear and exploit the hysteria and confusion."

Gasps and words of astonishment filled the room as water fills a tank. A harmonious roar drowned out all attempts to silence the audience for several minutes. The conversation died down and the visitor continued his report.

"Rumors of unnatural occurrences surfaced several days prior to my departure. It seems a small Carcalian village was

125

attacked by a Wild Pack of Tigrens. All were taken hostage except two inner-city traders. They contacted my Shandowl and a search party was sent out to investigate. Fourteen were sent out, only five returned alive. The two Carcalians that witnessed the demise of their village died at the scene.

We were organizing a strike force on the night of the attack, when all of a sudden arrows rained down on us. Bengal and I fled the castle when the warriors breached the outer walls and entered the courtyard. I'm only saddened that we were the only ones to escape in time.

We've come to you out of desperation. These fighters are swordsman and strike very tactically. We need a major army to put a stop to those beasts and reclaim our ancestral lands. We know, from the Great Games that you are the best of the sword masters. We humbly ask for your help."

"This is a most disturbing report," muttered Pensha, "we thank you for having the courage to make such a journey. We are most appalled at these occurrences and will certainly come to a swift solution to this alarming chain of events."

All but the highest of officials were dismissed from the meeting chamber. The High Council discussed the reports that were given, the possible solutions, and the possible ramifications of those solutions. There were many opinions flying back and forth about how to proceed, but the outrage in not surveying

126

Sphynxia and Raoolia came to the forefront of the discussions. The seed of danger goaded a few to propose a surgical infiltration of Raoolia to see first hand the cause of these strange occurrences.

The delegation was ushered back into the Council Chamber, along with Master Hann and Bengal.

"The committee has come to a solution about Raoolia," began Pensha. "We will send a surgical strike team to land on the continent and make a ground survey. As an extra measure of security, the strike team will have three vessels consisting of a battalion of backup troops waiting to come to their aid. We have a new, tactical weapon that we've been testing. The battalion will remain on the vessels, and if help is required, the weapon shall be fired into the air. The battalion will provide a barrier to allow the strike team to press on or retreat, depending on the circumstances."

Shou 112, 5049

All were dismissed. The warriors were briefed on their mission, and preparations were made for their fateful mission – to discover the Mystery of Raoolia!

Chapter 23: Mystery of the Red Rain

Shou 151, 5049

"Okay, if you don't hear from us by sundown, come ashore and retrieve us. I know this seems to be either a partial or total suicide mission, but if we're lucky, we'll all live to regret this moment," instructed Lieutenant Kahn.

The three vessels of two-hundred fifty troops anchored their boats along the western continental shelf of Raoolia. Suspicious minds queried the unusual edge of the forest, where the remains of a forest fire still lingered. Tigrens had the natural ability to zoom in on distant objects, an adaptation to hunting not yet lost in the genetic whirlpool.

The search team consisted of a squad of twelve soldiers. They fanned out in a triangular formation, to backup the leader and to cover more ground. The squad crossed the threshold separating The Land of the Dead and the shoreline. A mist began to swirl in, consisting of a dense, blue mass of cold air. The mist enveloped the squad, and out came the wraiths from all directions. Before the soldiers were able to defend themselves, the ghostly apparitions tore them apart like they were made of paper! Blood spurted and spattered in all directions! The mangled bodies were whisked upward on a breeze and were hurled into the upper atmosphere!

Shortly after losing sight of the team, a red mist rained from above on the troops stationed on the vessels, still anchored offshore. Moments later, their comrades' limbs, hair, and organs fell from the heavens! Decapitated heads bounced on the three decks and rolled to rest at the feet of each of the commanders in charge of the vessels.

"By the Grace of the Gods!" exclaimed Morndas. "What in the name of Cougran is happening!" he shrieked. Tattered clothing, boots, mangled weapons, and a strip of felinoid intestine were all Morndas needed to understand what had just stained their decks red. Their strike team was gone!

"Send for the other commanders! I want no more loss of life here! We will encircle the continent and meet on the eastern shore. Send for them at once!"

Dinghies were sent to the other two ships to retrieve their commanders. The two commanders arrived several minutes later. They boarded and the three leaders entered the galley to discuss the next step.

"There's no way we're going in there!" shouted Mahn. "We've lost twelve good Tiges! They didn't even have time to shoot off the signaler! Not to mention the fact that I now have entrails scattered all over my deck! No way am I sending any of my warriors in that way!"

"Calm down Mahn," stated Dougar in a dry tone. "No one is foolish enough to try that way. I suggest we split up and send a small team of five to each of the remaining shores. I'll sail around to the east. Mahn, you can take the south and Morndas the north."

"Agreed. This will minimize loss of life and accomplish our goal. Remember, at any sign of danger, disengage. If that's not possible, fire the signaler. We've stumbled upon something or someone that doesn't like visitors. We must be cautious," said Morndas.

"We'll meet here in 4 days and discuss our findings. I feel that this situation is much more complicated than we realize. Any more to add?" delivered Mahn. With a resounding shake of the head from both commanders, Mahn said, "Good luck to you both. Return safe, and alive."

The dinghies returned the commanders to their respective posts so the plans could be conveyed to their subordinates.

Shou 153, 5049

Dougar and Mahn sailed their vessels south, following the shoreline. Mahn's ship anchored off the south-central beach and dispatched their team to shore.

Shou 155, 5049

Dougar continued around the southern shore until he reached the southeast corner of the continent. He then shifted north and anchored after reaching an unusually rocky shore. He dispatched his team of five.

Shou 153-155, 5049

Morndas' crew noticed an unusual break in the forest. They also noticed that there was land where there should be water! The Straits of Raoolia were gone! But how? There were no geologic documentations of fault lines that could produce this phenomenon! One thing was for sure, those mysterious tidal waves were tied to this unnatural emergence of land. They continued to the north, which, they figured, was the north shore of Sphynxia. The boat swung east, anchored on the continental shelf, and sent their detachment to shore.

Many perils lie in wait for the unsuspecting Nidian soldiers. What will they find on New Raoolia? Only Master RRandoll knows for sure...!

Chapter 24: Raoolian Raid

Shou 154, 5049

The fireteam from Morndas' ship rowed to shore, full of anticipation of what may come to pass upon their arrival. As the beach grew closer, tension between the five scouts grew. At last, the moment of truth, the beach was beneath them!

The north shore of Sphynxia had white, sandy beaches for miles, as far as the eye could see! At the edge of the beach, a meadow stretched for miles in all directions. This, in turn, fed into what looked like the remains of a lush forest. The contrast between the meadow and the blackened trees was striking! The grassy meadow was alive with insects fluttering about amongst the tall, green grass and flowers. The forest, however, was deathly quiet, devoid of even insects, which pervade even the urban centers. The scorch-marks irregularly marked the trees at different heights, indicating a recent fire. The trees were strikingly the same when it came to leaves; all were devoid of them, even the upper canopy!

The team fanned-out in a classic V-formation, the base of the V being the first in line. They cautiously stepped up the sandy embankment to the grassy field, looking in all directions for signs of any threats. None were found, and the fireteam continued through the meadow and stopped at the edge of the blackened forest.

"It appears to be lifeless, not a bird or insect alive in that charred forest. Very peculiar. We should be cautious with our entry into this sanctuary of death," pronounced Shankall, sergeant of Morndas' fireteam.

Shou 155, 5049

On the eastern shore, Mahn's team met with a different situation: beautiful, sandy beaches at a gentle incline to a forest brimming with life. The edge of the forest could be seen in the distance, along with the Raoolen River, which by all accounts, should empty into the Sybeerian Ocean, but now is stopped by rocky, sandy soil.

They too fanned out in a V-formation, keeping watch in every direction for possible threats. Walking along, they had every eye and ear tuned to the slightest disturbance, with the exception of what was underneath their feet!

The troops, standing five feet apart from each other, didn't expect the forested area to fall out from underneath them, but that is exactly what happened! All of a sudden, three of the five scouts had fallen into an odd-set of depressions in the soft soil! The three fallen comrades shook their heads and picked themselves up out of the unexpected change in the land.

"Whoa! I've never seen a hole like this!" said Kappel, a professional land surveyor for the Clushpow Geological Society. "This is highly unusual for a forested floor. It must have been made artificially. But what, or why would such a hole be dug?" asking with great awe.

"Hey Kappel, why don't you get a better look at it from that tree? Maybe it's important," said Jonel, sergeant, and leader of the search team, in a mocking tone.

"Okay I *will*," he sneered. Within seconds, Kappel was sinking his claws into the bark of the fanshow tree, common to eastern shores. He climbed to a height of about 30 feet and looked down. What he saw surprised him so much that he lost his balance! Gravity overtook him and brought him crashing to the ground with a resounding thud! Seconds later, he was spitting out a mouthful of forest moss!

Shou 153, 5049

The southern shore of Raoolia was very hostile, feeling the resistance from gale force winds following the Straits of Raoonada, separating the two continents.

Dougar's vessel dropped a double anchor, and dropped its sails in order to keep from capsizing in the tumbling seas. The fireteam rowed ashore, and due to the extra strain from fighting the wind, they decided to build a fire and rest before exploring their stretch of land.

Night fell on the continent. The howl of the wind was non-stop. The team would be hard pressed to start early, assuming they could last the night.

The forest was alive with rumbles and cries from the various species that populated its confines. What lies in store for the three teams was dire, and the ultimate survival of Cougran lies in their hands.

The Guardians of New Raoolia
were stirred by the disturbances
that invaded their lands.
Master RRandoll's
Minions
of Darkness
will be tested against
the Master Swordsmen
of the
Clushpow Clan!

Chapter 25: Another Piece of the Puzzle

Shou 153, 5049

Marching in block-formation, the Minotaurs sighted a light source on the beach that broke through the pitch-black night. They sent two squads of ten to the beach to investigate this new presence on their land.

A faint series of thuds awoke one of the scouts out of a dead sleep. He turned his head to see a group of shadows moving toward them. He grabbed his flare gun and shot it into the pitch-black night. The explosion woke the other four team members.

"What's going on, Dall?" asked Penskar.

"Approaching from the northwest," he whispered, as he pointed toward the shadows that were moving rhythmically in unison, as if in a military formation.

Penskar turned in the direction Dall was pointing and ordered his warriors to prepare for battle. They all unsheathed their swords and braced for the assault, for now the shadows were moving at quite a clip!

Metal clanged with metal as the outnumbered Tigrens battled multiple opponents simultaneously! Rhythmic parries and blocks created an ensemble of bangs and clanks, along with a barrage of sparks from the swords making contact with the others' edge! After several minutes of dodging their attacks, Penskar ordered a hasty retreat from the pointless battle, knowing full well that this particular opponent was the one that wiped out the Shven-Shong. They distanced themselves from their attackers quite quickly, being several times more agile than the lumbering beasts. They boarded their boat and set off to the main ship, which was on full alert due to the signal flare.

The vessel received their scouts, pulled anchor, and departed east, to meet the others at the rendezvous point.

Shou 155, 5049

Kappel picked himself up off the ground, amidst a calamity of laughter from his colleagues.

"Are you finished?" he asked, after the snickering began to die down. "This hole is a footprint, and they face north, so whatever made them went that way."

After voting 3 to 2 for following the tracks, the scouts departed north, to discover what abomination could have been big enough to make such a track. The journey would be short, however, for the fireteam's scent had been picked up by one of Master RRandoll's *pets*!

Boom! *Boom!* **Boom!** ***Boom!*** BOOM! ***BOOM!***

The ground trembled under its gait! A massive beast with sharp, pointed teeth stopped before the fireteam! It angled its head downward to fully envelope the Tigrens with its gaze! It towered above them, its head parting the branches of the tallest of trees! No such animal had ever been reported, much less expected to be eyeing the five for lunch! The flare was fired, and the great beast backed up for a moment, startled by the noise! It let out a deafening roar that temporarily left the scouts shell-shocked!

The bellowing biped stood 60 feet tall, had an oval-shaped head, binocular vision, nostrils large enough for a Tigren's head to fit into, and three large, clawed toes, which were the same size as the track that they had discovered! The three-inch daggers that encircled its upper and lower jaws were menacing as they were sharp! Its front limbs were very short and looked useless, but its legs and teeth more than made up for them!

The crew made a mad dash for the sea to launch their boat to return to the main vessel. The beast began its chase, scooping its neck down, snatching a lingering scout in its jaws, and swallowing it in one huge gulp! Five departed for the ship, four made it back to the boat, but the creature was too fast. He was on top of the boat just as the scouts attempted to leave the shore! Those that weren't squashed were pinned by the gargantuan claws, and then eaten alive! The screams of the soldiers being consumed by the massive beast could be heard all the way to the anchored ship! The gory scene was witnessed by the whole ship, still anchored on the continental shelf. With heavy hearts, they pulled the anchors and set sail for the rendezvous point.

Shou 154, 5049

A blue mist of fog gathered in the charred forest on the north shore of New Raoolia. Even though the scouts hadn't crossed into The Land of the Dead, the wraiths began their entrance into the physical world.

"Hey, look at that! What is that?" asked Zant.

"What ever it is, it's getting closer. Let's back away. We don't want to end up in pieces on the deck of our own ship," ordered Shankall.

Zant grabbed a small rodent, who, unluckily, decided to run out of its burrow and right into the center of the group.

"Let's see if it'll attack." He threw the rodent into the fog, which hovered above the ground, and the rodent was caught by a skeletal hand, emerging from the blue mist! The rodent squealed and all of its hair fell out. Its skin turned bluish-white and it exploded! The hand retreated into the blue fog, waiting for the Tigrens to enter the cursed land.

The flare was fired into the air and a full retreat was ordered. The five scouts returned to their boat and rowed back to their vessel. The vessel turned toward the east and sailed to the rendezvous point.

Shou 161, 5049

The mystery of the convergence of Raoolia and Sphynxia had not only been deepened, but more questions arose on why it was so heavily guarded. From enormous predators to unstoppable warriors to mystical entities, the puzzle of Sphynxia and Raoolia had broadened. But while the quest to answer those questions only yielded more questions, one thing was for sure, another piece of the puzzle had been discovered. A new super-continent had caused the mighty tidal waves that destroyed hundreds of lives on three continents.

The rendezvous was met with a mixture of outrage, sadness, and determination. This expedition was successful in completing the original goal, but at the cost of several lives. Their departure ushered in some much needed relief and a significant decrease in stress. A foreboding report to the Nidian High Council would only escalate this already dangerous and disturbing chain of events.

Book 6: Invasion

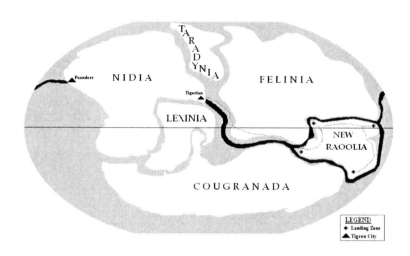

Chapter List:

Chapter 26:   Findings...   **142**

Chapter 27:   Inside the Nidian High Council.....................   **146**

Chapter 28:   Deployment...   **150**

Chapter 29:   Springing the Trap!..   **154**

Chapter 30:   A Mixed Victory...   **160**

Chapter 26: Findings

Ringlue 31, 5049

The six week journey back to Nidia was filled with outrage and mourning for the loss of their comrades-in-arms on the new super-continent. They arrived at Tigerian and mounted scout dragons to get to the High Council in record time.

Ringlue 34, 5049

The delegates were all summoned together before the Nidian High Council for the report on Sphynxia and Raoolia. The initial survey of the planet was thwarted by the arrival of Master Hann and Bengal. The delegation sent to the two continents was to discover the source of the tidal waves and verify the reports of a grave threat dominating the continent. The information they were about to receive would challenge the very foundations of what is real in this world.

"The High Council of the Continent of Nidia will now come to order. Delegates from the Sphynxian-Raoolian expedition are recognized and are to state their findings," announced Verdand.

"Thank you, Highness. We regretfully inform you that our news about the Raoolian Continent is rather grim," began

Morndas. "The initial landing on Raoolia produced total fatality. The landing party was attacked, dismembered, and hurled into the atmosphere by a spiritual entity. We know this because several of their heads came to rest on the decks our three ships. A red mist covered miles of water, which stained our ships red shortly before their heads came to rest at our feet."

"We must stop you, and order a moment of silence for our fallen brethren," said Pensha in a grim tone. The silence was held for several moments. Pensha said, "Please resume your report."

"I summoned the commanders of the other three vessels and we agreed to each take a coast. What we discovered was most disturbing.

On the north coast, like the west coast, the spiritual entity prevents any living being from crossing into its boundaries. A rodent was thrown into their domain and a skeletal hand emerged from the misty fog, caught it in mid-air, and destroyed it.

The east coast is guarded as well. At least one ferocious beast patrols the coast. This beast stands sixty-feet high, walks on two legs, and is one of the most menacing predators ever seen. We lost five Tigrens to its hungry jaws."

"For those five, I again ask for a moment of silence," repeated Pensha. "Do you have any more to report?" she asked, after several moments of respectful silence.

143

"Unfortunately, Highness, I do," replied Morndas.

"Please…go on," said Verdand.

"A ship was sent to the southern coast. Due to an excessive windstorm, the crew had a hard time fighting the current to get to shore. Upon their landing, they built a fire. That is what attracted them…the beasts spoken of by Master Hann of the Shven-Shong! Our scouts were able to out-maneuver them and return to their vessel, but they were quite the adversary.

The final bit of news that needs to be reported is that we discovered the origin of the massive tidal waves. Raoolia and Sphynxia are now joined where there was once open sea. The obvious border is lacking vegetation and littered with the remains of sedentary sea life that couldn't be carried off by the upheaval of water."

Shock and dismay filled the concerned Council Members as they absorbed this disturbing new information. It seemed that a grave threat has taken occupation of Sphynxia-Raoolia, and it would be up to the Nidians to stop this threat from growing.

"Thank you for your report, Morndas," said Verdand. "We will hear all view-points and decide what is to be done. All but the Council Members are dismissed."

Certainly, great care would have to be taken in any final decision regarding the new continent. All viewpoints and consequences must be considered before any action should take place.

The fate of all Carcalians and Tigrens everywhere will depend on sound judgment and total success.

Chapter 27: Inside the Didian High Council

Ringlue 34, 5049

The Council seemed to debate the issue for hours. Invading the continent was a clear violation of the jurisdiction agreements that the Clans had arranged. A question was raised about what the purpose of invading the continent would be, what there was to gain, and what would be the ultimate objective.

"We must capture one of their warriors in order to discover a weakness," shouted Dozak, a normally quiet Council Member. "These deaths are on our heads if we continue to allow this enemy to exist! We must take this issue head-on, and follow it to whatever conclusion that results! We have lost too many countrymen, not to mention an entire Clan!"

"But an invasion will most likely result in mass casualties, which is an unacceptable risk at this point," argued Rhinita. "However, I do agree that we should attempt another reconnaissance mission to capture one of their warriors. If it is true that they can regrow amputated limbs, then we need a specimen to study."

"I concur," agreed Pensk. We cannot defeat an enemy if we do not know its weakness. We must discover its concept of death and exploit it. The Shven-Shong were mighty warriors, strong in hand-to-hand combat. If they were wiped-out by these warriors, then we truly are facing a formidable foe."

"Let's put it to a vote. All in favor of sending a reconnaissance force to Raoolia to capture these warriors, raise your hands." Verdand counted eight in favor of the idea. "All opposed?" Verdand counted four. "Do you four dissidents have a different solution?"

"I think we should send a massive air strike to the continent with our archers, riding upon fire-breathers. Loss of life will be minimal if any, and perhaps then a ground force can be mobilized to secure the territory," proposed Sebel.

"I think the best thing to do is to contact the other Clans and work with them to gather more intelligence. We still don't know who's behind all of this. There may be an even graver threat pulling the strings behind the scenes," suggested Dozak.

"A better solution would be to try and contain the threat to Raoolia, station our sea-liners in and around the continent, so to contain the threat while we send a team in to capture one of the warriors for study," announced Clance.

"Much time has passed since the initial attacks. What makes you believe that this is a threat to our well-being? They could just want the two continents and nothing more. We don't have any reason to believe that they've destroyed the Ringlue

Clan, nor can we rule them out as suspects for these misdeeds. I say we wait and see what they will do next," said Salm.

"Anyone wish to change his or her vote?" asked Pensha.

"Well," began Elan, "these new options present an alternate point of view, and it would be wise not to discount them entirely. Perhaps a hybrid of all view-points that don't contradict is the way to go."

"You have a point," conceded Jone, "as with any conflict, there are multiple defenses to any offense."

"But we haven't concluded that this wasn't a defensive measure, and that our arrival wasn't seen as an assault! As with any conflict, there are peaceful solutions as well as aggressive ones. I am more in favor of peaceful ones," stated Salm.

"All in favor of creating a hybrid of the five opinions raise your hands. Any oppose?" asked Verdand. After the count, Verdand laughed to himself. These decisions always took place in the same way, yet the gravity of this particular situation seemed to escape the other members.

The vote for the hybrid plan won by just two votes, seven in favor to five against. The hard part was deciding to act, not what act would be done. More often than not, the vote not to intervene won the day, but not this day. It seemed that the

Nidians would be pulled into this headlong, and that action to this situation was the only solution that made sense.

Little did the Clushpow Clan know that this conflict was destined. No Tigren Clan in all of history had been more suited for the task than the Clushpow. They were the best at hand-to-hand combat. They were the most caring, and willing to help of any Clan. They felt that they were undefeatable when it came to any foe.

Master RRandoll felt a shift...he wasn't quite sure what it was, for he was still learning all the intricacies of the meteorite's power. Was it a major battle that he felt? Was it his demise at the hands of some unknown force? He wasn't sure. He knew he must be prepared for anything that may be coming on the horizon...

Chapter 28: Deployment

Ringlue 41, 5049

The signal for launch was given, and with sails taut and winds steady, the first fleet of Nidian warships set sail for New Raoolia. A battle fleet of warships from the east and west coasts, consisting of a total of five-hundred of the most sophisticated sailing vessels the Nidians had were launched to surround the continent of New Raoolia. Two-hundred fifty launched from Tigerian on the eastern peninsula and two-hundred fifty launched from the Tigren city of Paandorr on the west coast.

The continent would be surrounded so no inhabitants could escape. Each vessel was staffed with a battalion of 650 warriors. Once they were ashore, they would secure the perimeter of the continent. Their mission was to envelop the continent, destroy the threat, capture a few warriors alive, and go home. A simple mission, it seemed, to the ill-informed Navy.

Horns broke the rustling of the fire-breathers as the launch signal was begun. Thousands of dragon fliers took to the skies from Tigerian. Ten divisions of fire-breathers, about 200,000, were launched first, to discourage any threats in the landing zones on New Raoolia. After the threats were minimized and a base was established, a battalion of serpentine dragons, numbering eight-hundred, would be launched. They provided both aerial and land transportation. After all the serpentines were in the air, the pack dragons would be launched, which had excellent muscle structure for overland missions and were very large, up to 200 feet long. They were used mainly to deliver cargo and for intimidating local predators like tansors, which could possibly pose a threat to smaller dragons. Little did the dragon force know that the Raoolian tansors were three times the size they were supposed to be!

The massive flocks of dragons caused an artificial solar eclipse as they flew over the planet! Nothing in the entire history of Cougran had ever prompted such a massive use of resources! But the threat on New Raoolia was anything but ordinary. This was the largest scale movement of troops ever organized!

Ringlue 80, 5049

The ships formed a perimeter, the eastern fleet meeting the western fleet at the north and south ends of the super-continent. Thirteen landers per vessel with fifty soldiers each were lowered from each vessel into the churning waters, making simultaneous landfall en-mass!

Just as the naval troops made shore, the sky went black with aerial support! They circum-navigated the shore, splitting into four flocks (50,000 pilots each), setting up base camps on the southeast, northeast, north west, and south shores of the continent.

Master RRandoll was alerted to a huge disturbance in the life force surrounding his continent! He ordered all his minions into hiding, to wait for the right moment to strike! As troops landed on the beach, Minotaur Warriors, all 1.2 million of them turned to stone! The blue mist of the wraiths dissipated, the predasaurs hid themselves in the forest, the Tonias hid in the canopy, the sphinxes laid close to the ground in the bushes around the Temple, and the giant tansors retreated into their massive burrows! All traps were set and now all they would have to do is wait!

Ringlue 82, 5049

For two days, each flock took turns flying over New Raoolia, trying to flush-out any danger. They surveyed from the northeast corner to the southwest corner, then split in half and flew northeast. A small flight-squad spotted a clearing where Sphynxia had been, and an unusual building in the forest. The ten pilots landed to investigate the unusual structure.

The 70 sphinxes hiding in the surrounding jungle focused on the squad of Tigrens that had landed near the Temple. Master

RRandoll had given them strict orders to attack if the Temple was discovered, yet now he has instructed them to hide.

'What could he be up to?' thought Liotoch.

"Hey, what's that over there?" asked Benst.

"Where?" asked Deke.

"It looks like a statue, but why here, in the middle of nowhere?" said Benst, in shock.

"Come on, let's go check it out," said Deke.

Ringlue 83, 5049

The last of the troops crossed into the charred forest. A blue mist slowly enveloped them. All awareness of their setting was hidden in the accompanying fog…

Troops on the southern shore came upon the campsite left behind by the previous scouts. They noticed a group of perfectly aligned stone statues. The group approached with caution…

Troops on the southeastern shore investigated the ruined dinghy that had been ripped into splinters. No sign of Tigren remains were found. They continued up the embankment and into the forest, searching for the mysterious attacker…

153

Chapter 29: Springing the Trap!

Ringlue 82, 5049

"Look at that! It looks just like the creatures that Master Cronk described!" said Deggar.

"Why would a statue be out here in the middle of the jungle?" asked Deke.

"Maybe it has something to do with that building..." remarked Bantor.

"What building?" asked Gent, Deke, Deggar, and Benst in unison.

Just then, a roar bellowed from the wilderness that surrounds the Temple! The creatures leapt from the bushes and charged the Tigren soldiers! With shock and awe, the Tigrens readied for the assault! Seventy strange creatures were running at full speed toward the group of ten Tigrens that had landed near The Temple of the Four Sphynxes! How would they ever escape?!

The signal flare was shot into the air, and forty more pilots descended from the skies! Several pilots were pounced upon and mauled by the fanged creatures, or severely wounded by swiping claws. A lucky and agile pilot managed a back flip just as the sphinx had landed. He then moved in and with an arcing swipe of his sword, its head plummeted to the ground and the body tipped over, spilling the blood that had nourished the brain of this abomination. The head began to shrink, its features becoming more and more recognizable. It was a Carcalian! But how? The body reverted to its Carcalian form as well, and the shock and stunning horror made him drop his sword! Another sphinx recognized the opening and leapt upon the unsuspecting warrior, mauling and clawing his quivering body until the life was fully extinguished. That was the end of Deke.

Sphinxes fell in large numbers to the skillful swipes of the Tigren blade! Yet the Tigrens slowly were littering the ground along with their adversaries. A sphinx killed left a different looking corpse. This horror kept the casualties on even ground, but the finite number of sphinxes were destined to be overwhelmed by the highly skilled Tigrens, who, by this time, had turned the tide against the vicious beasts! When all was said and done, the ground was littered with 69 dead Carcalians and 25 dead Tigrens.

The sphinx formerly known as Liotoch watched as his entire village was slaughtered before his eyes! Master RRandoll, being in full control of his will, forced him to lay down in a hidden location away from the rest of the attacking sphinxes. They attacked and lost, which was foreseen by his Master, and the horror of watching the slaughter was imposed on Lio to inflict an ever-greater level of torture on the Carcalian who had invaded Denzcan's woods and started this whole affair!

The exhausted army fell to their knees, taking in the full extent of the event that had transpired. The corpses, maimed, clawed, mauled, beheaded, littered the ground, painting the landscape a reddish color that intensified the grief-stricken warriors. These abominations were kinsmen! When the grief was at its highest, and every warrior had dropped to their knees in sorrow, the Minotaurs, who had been lurking in the shrubs and overgrowth, bellowed their war cry and charged at the remaining invaders! All were stabbed, then bitten. The dead were also bitten, which dragged their souls from the spiritual realm and imprisoned them within the killing machines that had just wiped them out! The dead Carcalians were left where they were, fodder for the insects and scavengers to contend and fight over! An unworthy death for the hapless victims all witnessed and remembered by the lone survivor, Liotoch, the sphinx.

Ringlue 83, 5049

The stone statues on the southern shore resembled the warriors described by the remnants of the Shven-Shong. Some of the troops intermingled with the statues, their curiosity outmaneuvering their sense of apprehension. When the troops were overwhelmed with curiosity, and had lowered their guard, the warriors snapped to life and impaled the foolish troops that had gotten to close for comfort. Several Tigrens lay slumped in their own blood while the Minotaurs proceeded to attack the stunned remaining troops who had hung back and kept their curiosity in check.

A fierce hand-to-hand sword battle ensued. Those Tigrens that fell were bitten and infected with the virus. This rejuvenated their dying bodies as the virus replaced it with the fierce beast known as the *Minotaur*!

The southeastern company of soldiers traversed through the foliage, numbering about two-hundred. A series of thunderous tremors shook the ground, one right after another from deep within the forest! The soldiers froze where they stood to get a bearing on where the sound was coming from. Then they split into two groups and went toward the noise, which had now ceased, and attempted to surround it. They crept through the brambles that blanketed the forest floor, inching ever closer to where they suspected the creature was lurking. The canopy began to shift as the gigantic snout poked through the branches...

The massive beast poked its snout in view of the warriors, pushing its head far enough forward to get a good look at its quarry. Its jaws spread, bearing hundreds of daggers for teeth, and then the deafening explosion broke the silent anticipation! Swords dropped, as both hands were needed to drown out the monster's call! The ground shaking bellow forced the army to its knees in excruciating pain!

Two additional predasaurs, standing to either side of the one that was roaring, took the opportunity to leap from the trees onto the unsuspecting regiment! Those not crushed by the claws and immense weight of the creatures, or killed by flying debris were snatched-up by their razor-sharp jaws! A few in each platoon were lucky enough to get their bearings and run, attracting the attention of the pair of predasaurs that had leapt from obscurity. The two predasaurs followed the retreating soldiers out of the forest and toward their landing boats! The bellowing predasaur closed its jaws and retreated to its hidden bed within the forest, laying down, awaiting the next round of victims!

Ringlue 84, 5049

Despite the mass casualties that were piling up all across the island, more Tigrens continued to set foot on the continent, determined to defeat the foe that had proven tougher to beat than anticipated.

Master RRandoll grinned ear to ear, his eyes narrowing, gleaming from the series of slaughters that had gone in his favor.

Victory would not be swift, for the numbers that continued to land were doubling every minute, but victory would be his!

Thousands of troops had crossed into The Land of the Dead from the north and western most perimeters.

'It is time, my wraiths, to defend your Master! Show no mercy!!'

The signal was given to unleash their full wrath upon the soldiers! Arms were ripped out of socket, femurs were broken, knees were shattered, necks were broken, jaws were bent and ripped from living flesh! Weapons fell to the ground en-mass, mirroring the initial invasion. A red mist spread in all directions, turning the charred forest into a bloodstained landscape! When all the troops were a mangled conglomerate of raw meat, the flesh fell to the ground, left to stink and rot as a warning against entry!

Chapter 30: A Mixed Victory

__Ringlue 83, 5049__

The retreating platoons who had encountered the predasaurs were in hasty retreat as the lumbering beasts were in hot pursuit of the invaders! One by one, the fleeing soldiers were snatched up by the ever-hungry jaws of the stalking predasaurs. Their never-ending hunger was designed to keep them fierce and determined to consume, a useful trait for a predatory guard.

The lead soldier, beginning to tire from the pursuit, saw the beach, which gave him extra incentive to continue, despite being out of breath. He reached the landing vessel and waded into the water, trying to dislodge it from the shore. Several other soldiers emerged from the forest and climbed aboard, filling the landing vessel to capacity as the thunderous crashing of the pursuing beasts loomed ever closer!

Two landing boats managed to launch and make their way out to deep water, but a third was not so lucky. The massive bipeds converged on the landing vessel and gripped the soldiers head first, snapping their spines, swallowing their upper bodies, and crushing their only means of escape with their enormous weight! A flare was shot to signal danger, which caught the attention of a flock of fire-breathers.

They arrived too late to save the fleeing soldiers, but that didn't stop them from opening up on the reptiles and unleashing tunnels of fire from their throats! The beasts were caught off guard and doused their flaming torsos in the cool sea, emerging blackened and angry. The riders were dropped off and the dragons flew in and attacked the abominations, biting and clawing the throats of the howling predasaurs, like a horde of bats en-mass! The huge predasaurs frantically shook their heads in an attempt to free themselves from the attackers as another flock swooped in to spew fire into their eyes. That spray of fire proved to be too much, as the lumbering beasts crashed to the ground. Their blackened faces and burned nostrils were damaged from inhaling the flames. Their eyes slowly closed, and when their hearts stopped beating, their bodies returned to the ash from whence they came!

Cheers sounded from the large ships that lay witness to the battle that ensued on the southeastern shore! The morale boost was coupled with sorrow in the loss of so many kin. But the excitement of the returning soldiers who had survived the near death experience made for an adventurous evening of story telling! Those anxious to hear the tale crowded around the survivors, those not, lurked about the ship, wondering how significant this victory really was, since they lost 150 soldiers in the ruckus.

Representatives were gathered to spread news of the victory over the predasaurs, and the loss of men to the lumbering beasts. Their hope was that the mistakes that led to so many deaths could be avoided. Perhaps the tide could be turned against these adversaries and life could return to normal.

Ringlue 84, 5049

The delegates boarded their dragons, sitting behind their pilots, and took to the air at daybreak to spread news to the fleet of vessels surrounding New Raoolia. A consensus was reached amongst the commanders that a base would have to be secured on the continent so that information could be centralized and the many tendrils of this war could be coordinated.

As quickly as the delegates reported good news, reports of mass failures also poured in. The entire scope of this battle began to take shape. Thousands of Tigrens were missing or presumed dead.

Ringlue 87, 5049

When the victory on the southeastern shore had been fully communicated, the delegates returned to their ships. Thousands of soldiers had simply disappeared on the western and northwestern fronts. Soldiers had been wiped out by mysterious warriors on the southwestern front, and several flocks of fire-breathers were missing that had landed on the northern interior. A base must be established so concentrated efforts can make a dent in this ever-difficult conflict.

The day was a glorious day for Master RRandoll! He beamed with pride at the success of the wraiths, the demise of the sphinxes, the torture of Liotoch, the destruction of 150 invaders on the southeastern shore, and the newly acquired soldiers outside his Temple. He regretted the loss of two of his predasaurs at the hands of the invaders, but they were easily replaced unlike the losses experienced by the invaders! While he had over 1.2 million Minotaurs, herds of tansors and predasaurs, gaggles of Tonias, and hordes of wraiths, he had an underlying concern that the second act of this war may not fair as well.

Book 7: Retaliation

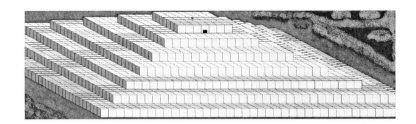

Chapter List:

Chapter 31:   Small Step Forward..   165

Chapter 32:   Voyage Home...   169

Chapter 33:   In the Navy...   173

Chapter 34:   Infiltration..   178

Chapter 35:   Out of the Woodwork...   182

Chapter 31: Small Step Forward

Ringlue 88, 5049

The commanders of all the vessels met in the war room of the flagship _Continental Quest,_ where Admiral Danterro was planning wave two of the invasion. Also present is the General of the Nidian Air Command, General Blaad, along with his wing commanders.

"We must lead a guerilla assault on the southern shore, sending both air and ground forces to break through the barrier and secure a base. Archers will accompany the air force to lay down cover fire on those soldiers. Absolutely no troops are to enter from the north or west, the charred forest has a powerful entity that we can't even fight, much less defend ourselves against. Our only hope is to enter quickly and leave quickly so they don't overwhelm our members. We still don't know what happened to part of our northern flock. It's imperative that we minimize the loss of life and maximize our effectiveness," stated Admiral Danterro.

The commanders were dismissed and teams from each ship converged on the southern shores. General Blaad directed his wing commanders to circle the landing team and serve as back-up should things go wrong.

The morning sky went black as the fire-breathers passed over head, approaching the Raoolian coast. Several landed and their riders gave the signal for the naval troops to come ashore. Five-hundred troops hit the sand running as their gangplanks lowered onto the shore. The troops fanned out in platoons of fifty, the archers ascended the trees at staggered altitudes, providing a back up force if the platoons needed to retreat.

Traps were set, such as snares, falling nets, and disguised trenches so that any patrols would be slowed down if the battle took a turn for the worse. Scouts crept through the thick overgrowth searching for fresh tracks, so that the current location of the beasts could be relayed to the soldiers.

The Minotaurs marched through the forest, alerted by Master RRandoll of a disturbance...

The scouts spotted the approaching squad of Minotaurs moving south toward their location. The scouts crept backwards and alerted the soldiers of the approaching squad. They sent a messenger back to the archers to get ready for the upcoming event. The archers readied their bows, waiting for the first hint of retreating Tigrens. The soldiers huddled close to the ground, waiting for the first signs of the beastly warriors.

"Attack!" shouted Commander Bahsheen.

The Tigren Army leapt out of the bushes that concealed their locations, kicking, stabbing, and fencing with the horned warriors. Arms were removed with a slash of the sword, and the stabbing blow to where the heart should be had no effect on the unnatural creature. With a backhanded slap, the Tigren who had impaled the Minotaur with his sword was knocked to the ground, flat on his back! The Minotaur removed the sword from his already healing body and removed the Tigren's head with one swift stroke of the Tigren's own sword!

"Close ranks and retreat!" announced Commander Bahsheen.

The Tigren Army retreated, drawing the Minotaurs through the malay of traps they had laid, avoiding the hidden trenches and tripwires with their natural agility.

The Minotaurs charged into the forest after the retreating soldiers. Nets fell entangling the beasts. Several fell into trenches and were impaled by sharpened branches. Those in the rear were able to avoid the majority of the traps; those leading the chase had been not been so lucky! Snares, designed to grab their feet and hang them upside-down reduced their numbers further.

The retreating Tigrens charged and crashed through the wilderness, alerting the archers positioned high in the trees. Only five Minotaurs had managed to avoid all the traps and come into full view of the waiting archers. Arrows began to bombard the five warriors, saturating them with hundreds of pointed projectiles. The highly skilled archers' arrows speared the Minotaurs' bodies, legs, and arms. None of the arrows even came close to stopping their pursuit, but the arrows that struck their legs slowed them just enough to allow the Tigren Army to net the Minotaurs! They then were able to disarm them and take them prisoner aboard their ship!

Aboard the flagship, the five Minotaurs were placed in chains inside a holding cell. It took over twenty Tigrens to secure them, during which several soldiers where stabbed by their razor-sharp horns. Relief set in after the final Minotaur had been secured.

Ringlue 89, 5049
With their primary mission accomplished, the flagship ordered the impenetrable perimeter of ships to remain as it sailed back to Nidia to deliver the Minotaurs for study.

If a weakness could be found, this war will come to a swift end, or so they thought.

Chapter 32: Voyage Home

Ringlue 89, 5049

The voyage back to Nidia, for once, was filled with celebration for the successful capture of the enemy combatants! The Minotaurs continuously pulled at their chains, kicked at the walls with their hooves, and bellowed in protest against their capture! Luckily, the chains were made of a Cougrinium alloy that was stronger than regular, pure Cougrinium. The walls, however, were less resistant to damage, and began to buckle and crack due to the consistent abuse.

Ringlue 91, 5049

After two days of constant damage, the chains broke free from the wall. The guards immediately alerted the Admiral of the situation, but were dismissed because they were in a holding cell.

"There's no way they're going to get out of that cell. Now stand-down," said Admiral Danterro. "But just to be safe, arm the guards with Felowitzers. Hit them with the weapons to control them the rest of the way home. That is all, Corporal."

"Aye, sir," he said, returning below deck to the holding pen, where the Minotaurs were attacking the walls in unison, trying to break through to the hull of the ship.

The sonic blasts from the Felowitzers hit the prisoners and they instantly fell to the ground, stunned by the high-pitched blast. Because Felowitzers disrupted the balance center in the brain and nerve signals in the body, there was no damage to the surrounding structure. The prisoners recovered quickly and snarled at their captors. They got up off the ground and began to stomp repeatedly, alternating each leg while looking the stunned guards directly in the eyes.

"Hit them until they stay down," said the Corporal.

The blasts continued every thirty seconds, each blast dropped the beasts flat on their backs. In predictable unison, they got up and resumed their stomping.

Master RRandoll felt the excruciating pain associated with the repeated assault of the Felowitzers on his minions. How could they have been taken without his knowledge? Why was he feeling the pain associated with the repeated blasts from the Felowitzers? The previous injuries that his minions have suffered had not affected him. He sent out the command to turn to stone, and the pain ceased. If his minions come in close proximity to their Tigren captors, however, they'd immediately snap to life and attack!

The stomping ceased as one by one the Minotaurs stood at attention and turned to stone. The act was completely overwhelming to the crew, for they had never seen a living creature mineralize before their very eyes! Not a word was uttered amongst the entire crowd of witnesses that had accumulated in anticipation of an escape attempt.

Finally, Corporal Pedur, who had ordered the immobilization of the captives said, "Keep a vigilant eye on these creatures. No one is to touch them until we reach shore. Is that understood?"

"Aye," the guards said in unison.

"The rest of you, back to your posts. We don't need an army to guard a few statues," ordered Corporal Pedur.

The voyage continued onward to Tigerian to deliver the captives of Raoolia to the High Council for study. The Minotaurs remained encased in their mineral prisons, just barely aware of their surroundings.

"Have they moved?' asked Private Donnd.

"No, they haven't moved in over a week," replied Private Sucarn.

"Do you think they're even alive?" asked Private Donnd.

"I don't know what they are. Regrowing limbs, instant healing of wounds, turning to stone, I just don't know what to make of 'em!" exclaimed Sucarn.

"Yeah...," was the only reply the mystified guard could make.

Ringlue 127, 5049

Guards rotated every three hours, to make sure that the remaining duties that needed to be tended to on the ship were kept up. After traveling for six weeks, land was sighted, and the Great Port of Tigerian came into full view!

Corporal Pedur and ten of his best Marines followed him down to the holding area. It was time to transport these prisoners and he was sure that it wouldn't be very easy.

"Open the cell doors and shackle their hands and feet. We'll then shackle them all together to avoid any running off into the wilderness," instructed Corporal Pedur.

The cell door opened and two guards approached the first stone Minotaur. They got within a foot away and the creature snapped to life! He bit both guards and charged the other eight surrounding Corporal Pedur. The guards drew their weapons and braced for impact.

"I knew this wouldn't be easy," said Corporal Pedur.

Chapter 33: In the Navy

Ringlue 127, 5049

Eight swords pierced the beastly abomination, right through the mid-section of his body! In the ultimate act of defiance, the vicious creature pushed the swords deeper and tried to bite his assailants! The unnoticed victims of the Minotaur's initial attack metamorphosized into two additional Minotaur Warriors and released the cell doors of the other four captives. The six of them charged the Corporal and his eight guards, bit them, and waited for them to complete their physical change. The fifteen Minotaurs systematically and successfully sought out the remaining members of the ship and infected each and every member, including Admiral Bahsheen. By the time the vessel was ready to dock, the Minotaur Army was in full control of the ship!

The *Continental Quest* was greeted by a host of dockworkers. When the gangplank was lowered, ten Minotaurs raced down the plank and leapt onto the dockworkers! They pinned their victims to the ground, biting them one after another! In short order, the 10 Minotaurs had a small platoon of their own and they set off to conceal themselves in the dark alleys of the city. The *Continental Quest*, loaded with over 200 Minotaurs, left the dock and began sailing back to New Raoolia. The

173

Clushpow's plan had failed! The Minotaurs were ordered back to New Raoolia to systematically rid themselves of the blockade, one ship at a time if necessary.

The ship was unequipped for ship-to-ship combat, but weapons were aboard in abundant quantities for hand-to-hand combat. The Minotaurs readied themselves for the six-week voyage home by sparring with each other and organizing segmented divisions.

Master RRandoll beamed with pride! Only five Minotaurs were needed to overcome an entire ship! Now he had a naval vessel at his command! Before long, he would have a fleet of ships to spread out from this confining equatorial continent, filling the world with legions of Minotaur Warriors!

Ringlue 166, 5049

The *Continental Quest* drifted on the wind, following the currents southeast. After six weeks of travel, the horizon filled with distant ships, and behind those ships was the homeland. The north shore was just around the bend...

The Minotaurs lowered dinghies into the choppy sea, filled with Minotaurs with grappling hooks on their crossbows! The dinghies, each having five Minotaurs, went to three ships, shooting their grappling hooks on the rims of the anchored vessels.

Several thuds were heard off the starboard bow. The deck officer turned toward the noise and saw a grappling hook fixed to the railing of the upper deck.

"We're being boarded! All soldiers on-deck! All soldiers on-deck!" shouted Deck Officer Enga.

The Minotaurs climbed the ropes up the ship's hull onto the deck, all being met by Clushpow sword-masters!

The battle began, one after another, swords were met with the ping of other swords, feet flailing about, trying to knock their attackers backward. Cougrinium met with flesh, and blood painted the deck a grisly red, as one soldier after another went down. All were bitten, all metamorphosized, and the ranks of Minotaur Warriors exploded! This ship was also in Master RRandoll's command!

The other two vessels fell shortly thereafter, and now there were four vessels under Master RRandoll's command! Dinghies were launched from those ships with Minotaurs armed with grappling hooks to board the remaining battleships. By day's end, the entire blockade had been taken! The RRandollian Navy was born!

<u>*Ringlue 167, 5049*</u>

Master RRandoll used his power to create ship-to-ship weapons. He commanded his Minotaurs to go ashore and transport them to his new naval vessels. The new weapons consisted of catapults, metal spears, giant crossbows to hurl the spears, reinforced ramming materials, and additional hand-to-hand weapons and grappling hooks for additional hostile takeovers.

<u>*Ringlue 169, 5049*</u>

When the ships were finished with their mass upgrades, they sailed outward to the other continents. It was time to spread out and introduce himself to the world!

'The Nidians will be the hardest to conquer, for they would have the most knowledge and the greater forces. The rest of the world will fall first, then, in massive numbers, the invasion of Nidia! This planet will me mine! Every living being will submit to my will! Success is only a matter of time, and time is on my side!' schemed Master RRandoll.

The southern flock of fire-breather pilots saw their ships begin to depart. The flock commander sent a scout to investigate, for the battle hadn't even been won, much less begun, as far as he was concerned. As the scout drew closer, the reason for their departure became ever apparent!

Chapter 34: Infiltration

Ringlue 169 – Shenlowpow 55, 5049

'A little detail I've overlooked. No matter,' thought Master RRandoll, seeing through the eyes of his Minotaurs.

The fire-breathers on shore saw their scout circle as a spear was hurled from one of the ships, missing the skillful pilot. The scout swooped in on the Minotaur-controlled vessel and spewed fire at its mainsail. The sail went up in a ball of flames! The ship's speed slowed as the sail turned to ash. More spears were projected into the air, none meeting its target.

"Mount-up, we've got a battle to win!" shouted the Commander Candowl. With their wings raised and tails out, the dragons leapt into the air one after another. By the time they reached the ship, the vessel was engulfed in flames!

"Split off and check out the other boats in the fleet," shouted the commander. "Attack at will! Send those ships to the bottom of the sea!"

Success for the Clushpow came when the first vessel began taking on water. The Minotaurs, unable to swim, were carried to the bottom of the sea. The crushing pressure of the deep sea immobilized the army and forced them into their mineral states, to avoid total destruction. They would remain at the bottom of the sea until Master RRandoll saw fit to retrieve them from their watery graves.

The remaining squadrons of the southern flock attacked the ships in full force. The crowded airspace made for easier targets, as the crossbows launched their giant spears into the congestion. Dragons plummeted into the sea, impaled by the barbed Cougrinium harpoons. Sails were ablaze along the entire horizon, and as the sun set on the 13 hour day, the flaming sails acted like floating torches, occasionally being quenched by the sinking of the ships into the dark, murky depths. The occasional splash was only noticed by the disruption of water, illuminated by the blazing boats.

Overall, 60 ships lay at the bottom of the sea and over 200 dead dragons drifted in the currents, some of them eventually washing up on shore. The Tigren pilots were able to swim to shore, the sun rising on their exhausted bodies on the sandy beach. The pilots eventually retreated as the sun began to rise, their numbers dwindling fast. This victory belonged to Master RRandoll's Navy.

The remaining 440 ships that had been conquered by the Minotaurs continued on to the continents they intended to invade. Minotaurs first landed on southern Felinia and northeastern Cougranada. They eventually invaded Felinia from the south, east, and western shores. Additional ships continued onto the eastern shores of Lexinia, and the southern shores of Taradynia.

Because a Minotaur has touched-down on the eastern shore of Nidia, and immediately began 'recruiting' additional Minotaurs, there was not need to send ships to the eastern shore. That small force would be needed to establish a foothold in the final act of Master RRandoll's sinister scheme!

Shenlowpow 1, 5049

"Any reports from the leaders of the invasion?" asked Master Cronk to Danjo, the Minister of the Docks.

"No sir. A ship pulled-up a day ago, but immediately returned to sea. No one has checked in and no scouts have been sighted in the air," replied Danjo.

"Most disturbing. Isn't it standard protocol to send a representative to check-in with the Dock Minister upon arrival?" asked Master Cronk.

"Yes sir. That's what's so strange. There has never been a returning ship that has arrived and departed within minutes. Supplies are always needed, or soldiers are homesick and need shore leave. They usually send in a scout, but nothing has been relayed concerning the naval or aerial invasion," he said.

"Gather a squad to scour the streets. There has to be someone out there who saw something. Given what the strike force is up against, I wouldn't put anything past this enemy," instructed Master Cronk.

"Right away sir," replied Danjo.

Master Cronk went to the staging area where the serpentine dragons had been gathered. They were still waiting for information from the first wave that a base had been established. He requested that the commander of the second wave of the invasion to meet with him concerning the progress of the war.

"Any news from the first wave?" asked Master Cronk.

"No sir. We've had no returning vessels nor incoming fire-breathers return with news," replied Commander Dank.

"Hmm...strange that we've received no word," Master Cronk said, thinking of what to do while pulling at his whiskers. "Send out your fastest dragon scout to find out what's going on. We need all the information we can get about the war front. So far, there was a report of a vessel landing at the docks, but no message has been received. Instruct the scout to be cautious. It is possible that this enemy has gained control or destroyed our fleet. If the fleet is sighted, approach it with great care."

"We will approach this with extreme caution, sir. I will send two, one to try and make contact, the other to observe and report back," said Commander Dank.

Chapter 35: Out of the Woodwork

Ringlue 82, 5049

Liotoch stood up on all four of his legs and moved into the clearing around the Temple, where the rotting flesh of his brothers lay scattered as far as the eye could see. Tigren and Carcalian corpses littered the landscape, the stench of rotting flesh destroying the natural perfume of the forest.

Now there was nothing to go back to. The city where he had come from was no more, all of his people were now slaves, his neighbors from BellBour had been slaughtered before his eyes, and he was imprisoned in this wretched body, himself enslaved to the will of pure evil. He had to do something with the carcasses of his fallen brethren, and since he no longer had hands to make fire with, he decided to dig a hole and bury them.

Shenlowpow 1, 5049

The retreating dragon-fliers who had not been successful in stopping the ships' departure for lands unknown, regrouped with the Tigrens who had washed up on shore. The defeat was a severe blow to the morale of the dragon-fliers, naturally arrogant because of their hit-and-run fighting style.

"How many lost in the assault?" asked one pilot.

182

"We're still trying to determine that," replied Sanchen. "Some pilots were swept away in the currents and others succumbed to hypothermia and drowned."

"This enemy is truly an adversary worth noting in the historical record. I fear this planet will only see more of this enemy. We must regroup and head toward the interior to find the mastermind behind this mayhem," said Lieutenant Zamborra.

After the dead had been collected from the ones that washed to shore, the pilots dug a mass grave and buried the deceased pilots and dragons together. A moment of silence was allowed for the dead as the pilots mounted their fire-breathers and headed north. They made sure to avoid the charred forest to prevent an encounter with the wraiths.

Foreign dragons passed into the interior of the continent on an intercept course for the Temple, based on their heading. Master RRandoll unleashed his Tonias...

Shenlowpow 3, 5049

Dragons suddenly began tumbling from the skies as the Tonias leapt from the trees, into the air, and directly at the belly of the fire-breathers! They rammed into them, knocking them from side to side, but not wavering their course. When full-throttle interception didn't change their course, the Tonias came about in droves against the dragons like a swarm of insects. They latched onto the dragons, burying their sharp teeth into their hides, trying to make them land. A few succeeded, sending a small number of dragons down through the canopy and onto the ground with a resounding crash, shaking the land for miles!

The Tonias, unscathed in the landing, began climbing their soon-to-be prey to attack the unconscious pilots. A roar in the distance, though, ceased their assault, and the Tonias who had ridden the plummeting dragons fled to the sky.

A distant roar woke the pilots from their state of unconsciousness. With blood-dried eyelids, the pilots used every ounce of energy they had to get off their deceased dragons to escape from what roared to the northeast. They hobbled northwest to leave the predators with a larger meal than themselves.

'They must not reach the Temple. Their invasion of my domain must be met with severe consequences...' the sound of Master RRandoll's commands resonated within his minions. The drakells were called into action...

The creatures that had caused the Tigren pilots to run into the wilderness came upon a feast in their desolate territory.

Dragons were highly prized by the Raoolian predators, for they would scavenge a carcass just as soon as they'd produce one. The hooks of the 30-foot tansors ripped through the tough hide and exposed the soft flesh below. The most prized portions were eaten first, the heart, for it was 3 feet in diameter, and the wing muscles, located in the back and the upper shoulder.

The fleeing Tigrens ran though the forest, trying to head in the direction of their comrades. They reached the river, which they presumed to be the Raoolen, and quenched their thirst with the cool, clean water. A pair of eyes spotted them from above, unbeknownst to the fleeing soldiers. The branches of the tree slowly parted. The Tonia drew closer to discover that his quarry had not escaped after all, they were right below cooling themselves in the river!

The pilots noticed they weren't alone when a cloud of fire shot past one as it flew over the treetops.

"Someone doesn't want us here!" said the pilots.

"That can only mean we're going the right way…"

__Epilogue__

Lieutenant Zamborra has sent a small flight-squad of fifty of his best fire-breather pilots north to discover the secrets hidden on Sphynxia. Little does he know what lies in wait!

Liotoch has experienced the worst horror he could possibly experience, having seen his brethren decimated by their own people, not being able to do a single thing to help! After burying his Tigren and Carcalian brothers, he returned to the forest, exiling himself from contact with any living being. His grief had destroyed his will to fight, sending him into an ever-sinking chasm of blackness...

Puven, Wensha, Babbel, Fent, Teelor, and Sando, after becoming useless after the March on Shalou City, were corralled by Rrondoxia, Master RRandoll's drakell, to the cave, where the Minotaur Generals promptly turned to stone. They would forever be entombed in this mineralized state. Vegetation arose to conceal the cave from any who might pass through this part of the forest...

Master Hann and Bengal have been sequestered in an undisclosed location in one of the several Clushpow Castles on

Nidia. The legacy of the Shven-Shong Clan rests solely in their surviving this war.

Master RRandoll, having deployed his Minotaur Army worldwide, now sits on his throne, waiting until his minions are in position. The meteorite's power has all but consumed the Tigren formerly known as Denzcan. He created a whirlpool in which he is able to gaze upon the world, as seen through the eyes of his subjects. As each day passes, the meteorite's power reduces Denzcan's body to deteriorated bones, rotting tendons, dissolving ligaments, all hidden by the cloak provided to him by the mysterious wraiths.

The wraiths, living between the spiritual and physical worlds, exist outside of time and can see events yet to come, the territory changes, the atrocities, the horrors, and the resolution to the war, all hidden to Master RRandoll.

More would be explained, he reasoned, as the war engulfed all the continents of Cougran. But for now, he must wait until all his pawns are in place…

To Be Continued in
The Adventures Beyond New Raoolia…

Appendix

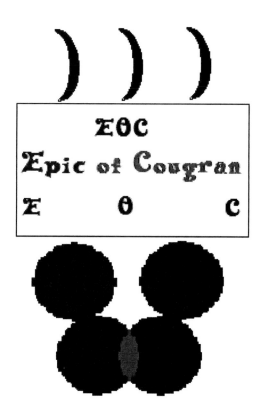

The Shougren Calendar

Month Name												
1	2	3	4	5	6	7	8	9	10	11	12	13
14	15	16	17	18	19	20	21	22	23	24	25	26
27	28	29	30	31	32	33	34	35	36	37	38	39
40	41	42	43	44	45	46	47	48	49	50	51	52
53	54	55	56	57	58	59	60	61	62	63	64	65
66	67	68	69	70	71	72	73	74	75	76	77	78
79	80	81	82	83	84	85	86	87	88	89	90	91
92	93	94	95	96	97	98	99	100	101	102	103	104
105	106	107	108	109	110	111	112	113	114	115	116	117
118	119	120	121	122	123	124	125	126	127	128	129	130
131	132	133	134	135	136	137	138	139	140	141	142	143
144	145	146	147	148	149	150	151	152	153	154	155	156
157	158	159	160	161	162	163	164	165	166	167	168	169

The planet Cougran takes 2,197 13-hour days to make one revolution around its blue-white star. Therefore, each year is sub-divided into 13 months, each being 169 days in length. The first seven months are named in honor of the seven Tigren Clans that have populated the planet. The 13 months of the year are:

1. **Shou** – Paw. Shou refers to the clan that all Tigren Clans originate, the Shou Clan. They invented the calendar and claimed the first month. They reside on the continent of Cougranada.
2. **Ringlue** – Fire. The Ringlue Clan occupies Sphynxia.
3. **Shenlowpow** – Unity. The Shenlowpow Clan occupies Felinia.
4. **Shven-Shong** – Chain-Claw. The Shven-Shong occupy Raoolia.
5. **Clushpow** – Claw-Sword. The Clushpow occupies Nidia.
6. **Svintz** – Flier, wing, or bird. The Svintz Clan occupies Taradynia.
7. **Maestry** – Shield. The Maestry Clan occupies Lexinia.
8. **Estrella** – Life. This month is when the Intercontinental Games and the Carcalian mating ritual occur.
9. **Danch** – Bone.
10. **Fwoo** – Fur.
11. **Fwooden** – Bear.
12. **Svintzshen** – Ground-dwelling bird.
13. **Scalint** – A bipedal reptile.

The days of the week are not named. Each day of the month has its own number. For example, the date for the first day of the year 5049 is written as Shou 1, 5049.

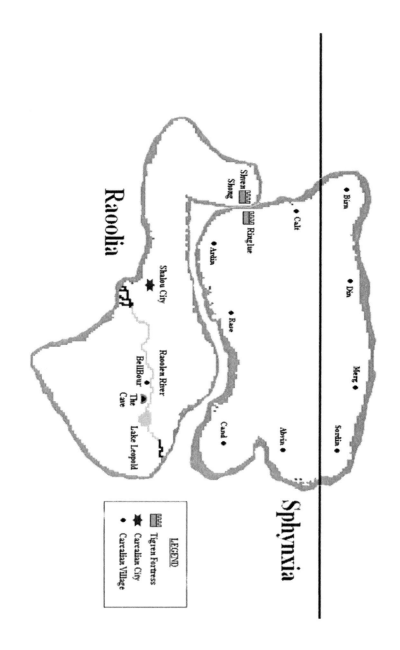

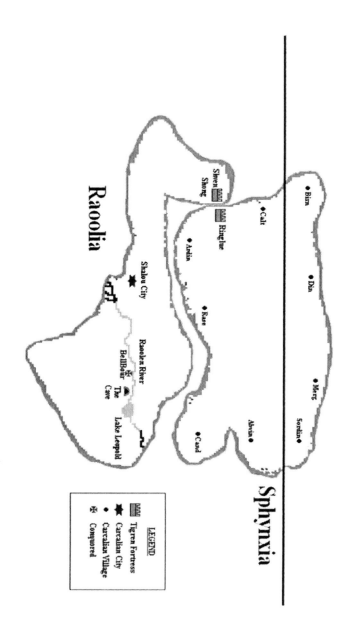

Raoolia

Sphynxia

Shwa Shong

Ringlue

Calt

Andin

Ruse

Shalou City

Raoolea River

Bellbour

The Cave

Lake Leopold

Birn

Dan

Merg

Alvin

Sordian

Cand

LEGEND

Tigren Fortress

Carcalian City

Carcalian Village

Conquered

VIII

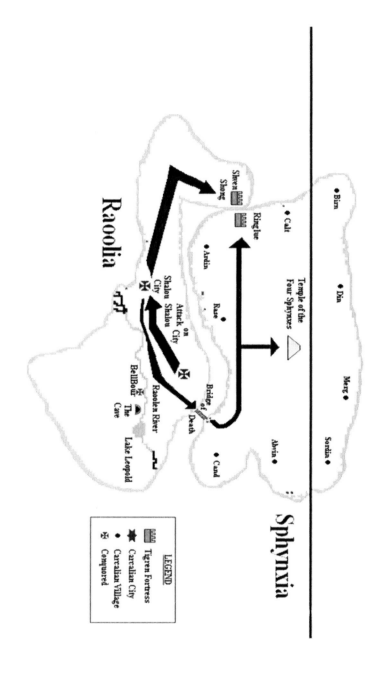

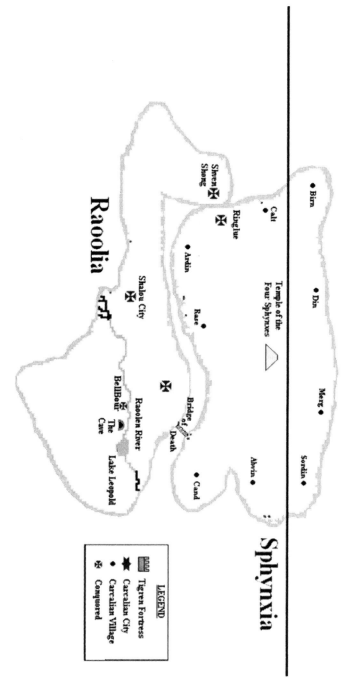

Raoolia

Sphynxia

Shwen
Shong

Cali

Birn

Ringlue

Ardin

Din

Shshu City

Rase

Temple of the
Four Sphynxes

Merg

Sordin

BellBeur
Cave

Raolen River

Bridge of
Death

Abrin

The
Cave

Cand

Lake Leopold

LEGEND

Tigren Fortress

Carzalian City

Carzalian Village

Conquered

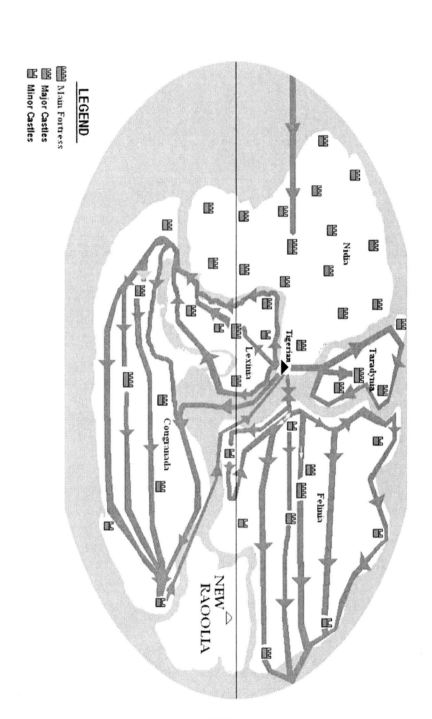

LEGEND

Main Fortress
Major Castles
Minor Castles

Nidia

Tigerian

Lexuna

Taradyna

Felina

Conguanada

NEW
RAOOLIA

XIII

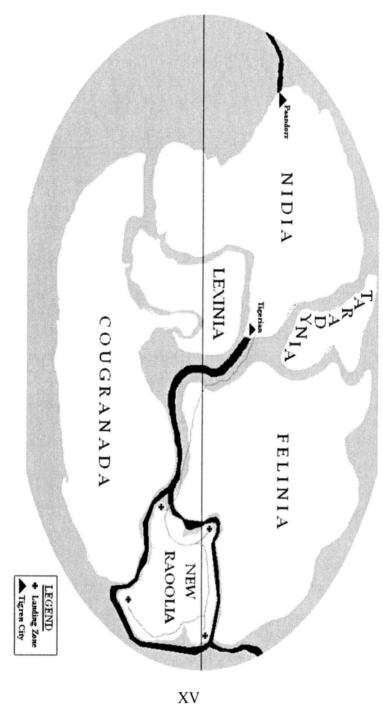

XV

XVI

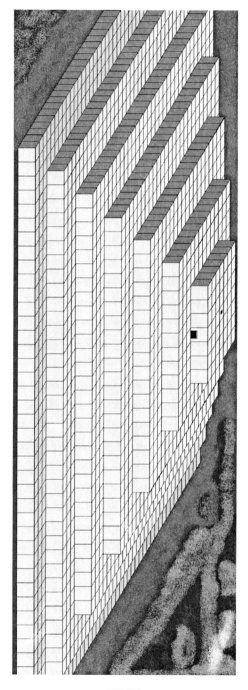

XVII